W9-BLZ-395

WITHDRAWN

Solimar

THE SWORD
OF THE
MONARCHS

Solimar

THE SWORD
OF THE
MONARCHS

by PAM MUÑOZ RYAN

DISNEY • HYPERION   LOS ANGELES   NEW YORK

Copyright © 2022 by Disney Enterprises, Inc.

All rights reserved. Published by Disney • Hyperion, an imprint of
Buena Vista Books, Inc. No part of this book may be reproduced or
transmitted in any form or by any means, electronic or mechanical, including
photocopying, recording, or by any information storage and retrieval system,
without written permission from the publisher. For information address
Disney • Hyperion, 77 West 66th Street, New York, New York 10023.

First Edition, February 2022
10 9 8 7 6 5 4 3 2 1
FAC-020093-21351
Printed in the United States of America

This book is set in Bembo Pro Italic, Chesterfield Std, Wingdings Regular/
Monotype
Designed by Shelby Kahr
Illustrations by Jacqueline Alcántara

Names: Ryan, Pam Muñoz, author.
Title: Solimar : the sword of the Monarchs / by Pam Muñoz Ryan.
Description: First edition. • Los Angeles : Disney-Hyperion, 2022. •
Audience: Ages 8–12 • Audience: Grades 3–7 • Summary: On the eve of her
Quinceañera, Princess Solimar discovers that it will take more than magic to
save her kingdom and prevent the destruction of the Monarch butterfly.
Identifiers: LCCN 2021007545 • ISBN 9781484728352 (hardcover) •
ISBN 9781368009966 (ebook)
Subjects: CYAC: Princesses—Fiction. • Sex role—Fiction. • Magic—Fiction.
• Monarch butterfly—Migration—Fiction. • Butterflies—Fiction.
Classification: LCC PZ7.R9553 So 2022 • DDC [Fic]—dc23
LC record available at https://lccn.loc.gov/2021007545

Reinforced binding
Visit www.DisneyBooks.com

~ To princesses and kings ~

Julia Ryan, Lila Abel, Benjamin Ryan, William Abel,
June Ryan-Retzlaff, and Hope Ryan-Retzlaff

ONE

The Arrival

Once, a rich and glorious Mexico stretched from the isthmus of the middle Americas to the northern redwood forests and as far east as the bayous. Within this vast land, one of twelve provincial kingdoms—San Gregorio— lay nestled in a highland valley bordered by thousands of oyamel fir trees.

Solimar, almost out of breath, ran toward the forest, hoping she wasn't too late. In one hand, she clutched a red silk rebozo, the tails of the finely woven shawl trailing behind her. In the other, she held a crown of flowers that she'd just finished weaving from pink dahlias, a swag of ivy, and ribbons. When she'd heard the news that the arrival was imminent, she dashed from the garden, calling to her grandmother, "Abuela, they're coming! I will meet you at the creek!"

Lázaro, a resplendent quetzal, flew alongside her, whistling and cooing.

"Yes, Lázaro," she told the bird. "I'm sure. A spotter in the tower saw the first wave headed this way and sent me a message."

Lázaro darted back in the direction from which they'd come, chittering loudly, his long tail feathers in a wild flutter.

"Oh, for heaven's sake! Don't scold me. I'm not completely without a chaperone. Abuela will be along soon. Besides, you know how she dawdles. And I don't want to miss the spectacle!" Solimar shaded her eyes and looked up.

In the distance, a dark veil surged and rippled.

She hurried along a footpath leading to a wide creek and stopped at the water's edge. On the far bank, the oyamel firs towered. "There—the sacred place!"

Like everyone in the kingdom, Solimar believed that the ancestors of the monarch butterflies inhabited the oyamel forest, and that year after year, their spirits lured a new generation of butterflies to this spot to rest during their migrations. In San Gregorio, the forest and the monarchs were revered and protected.

For as long as Solimar could remember, she had come to the woods to greet the first wave of butterflies on their journey.

She was forbidden to come alone or to cross the creek, which was riddled with rocky outcroppings and notorious currents. Everyone in the kingdom feared the rushing water that often dragged wayfarers downstream.

Even so, she'd always wanted to sit in the midst of the butterflies as they arrived. She couldn't do that on *this* side of the water. Solimar paced. "You know, Lázaro, I'm not a little girl anymore. I shouldn't have to wait for a chaperone. Besides . . ." She placed the crown of dahlias on her head and straightened her shoulders. "I'll need to be courageous someday. Why not start today? I give myself permission."

Lázaro shook his head.

Solimar tied the rebozo around her waist and leaped. She landed on a rock surrounded by swirling water and wobbled back and forth. "Whoa . . ." With both arms outstretched, she found her balance.

Frantic, Lázaro flapped his wings in warning and chirruped.

"You don't have to be such a mother hen!" she said, jumping from stone to stone, each one larger than the last. "Just a few more . . ." She hopped to a cluster of boulders midstream. On the tallest, decades of gushing water had created a tapered crevice through the rock.

"Look, Lázaro. The gap is an image of a sword! And the pommel at the top of the hilt is a porthole." She peered into the oval opening and saw a cameo of the forest on the other side. "I can fit my hand through to steady myself. It's the perfect holding-on place." She swung to the other side of the boulder, lowering herself onto a rock submerged in the water.

The bird tugged on her skirt.

"So what if my boots get a little wet? There's no going back now." She gingerly took a few more steps until she reached the far bank.

Scrambling to a shady spot between two trees, Solimar considered the tall firs and muttered, "I'd climb them if I could reach the lowest branches and if I was wearing trousers." Instead, she sat cross-legged on the forest floor. She untied the rebozo, flipped it over her shoulders, and straightened her crown.

Above, a kaleidoscope of butterflies quivered.

Lázaro flew to her side and burrowed beneath the drape of the rebozo.

Her dark brown eyes were wide with awe; she grinned, and her cheeks dimpled. "It's happening. . . ."

As the monarchs descended, the flutter of thousands of wings pitter-pattered like gentle rain. They landed on branches, swarmed around the oyamel firs, or drifted to the creek to drink, the water trembling from the beating of wings.

She sat as still as she could. As one after another perched upon her, Solimar's heart raced. She lifted a finger and several monarchs rested on it. This close, she could see the shimmering scales on their wings. "Buenas tardes. Welcome to San Gregorio. I want to reassure you that my family and I will do

— PAM MUÑOZ RYAN —

everything in our power to protect the forest so you'll always have a home. It's a solemn promise."

Lázaro peeked from beneath the folds of the rebozo.

"Come out and greet them," encouraged Solimar.

A butterfly landed on Lázaro's head.

Dozens covered Solimar. One landed on her face. The light touch felt like the tickling of feathers. When she giggled, the monarch burst upward, then slowly settled upon her again.

Lázaro inched forward and perched on her knee. He lifted one wing, then the other, and held still until the butterflies fluttered down to roost on him, too.

"Isn't it amazing that the butterflies, who have never been here before, arrive season after season at the same spot as their ancestors? Is it the magnetic pull of the earth or the position of the sun, as the scientists suggest? Or do the spirits of their fathers and mothers whisper directions to them in a dream? Is it some magical intuition that allows them to know what lies ahead? Any way you think about it, Lázaro, it's a miracle!"

Lázaro, now completely covered in butterflies, made a high-pitched warble, and his new friends took flight.

"You're right. It's also a mystery. Still, I wish *I* knew what came next. Imagine always knowing in your heart which way to turn and what life has in store for you around the next corner." As Solimar carefully stood, Lázaro flew to a nearby branch.

She held the ends of the rebozo outstretched so that the

fabric hung beneath her arms. The butterflies remained attached, even as a final trail of stragglers slowly drifted down and landed on the rebozo, too.

"I have giant wings made of butterflies!"

As Solimar slowly turned in a circle, a sunbeam pierced through the swordlike crevice in the boulder from the creek, spotlighting her. She tilted her face toward the warmth and, for a moment, closed her eyes.

A rhythmic humming surrounded her. Her eyes flew open, looking for who might be nearby. Yet there was no one. Where was the sound coming from? Was it the wind? Was it the monarchs? Or just her imagination? She laughed. "Lázaro, is it just me? Or did you hear ancient chanting?"

Lázaro shrugged and preened.

She closed her eyes again, and the chorus continued. For some reason, though, she wasn't afraid. Instead, she was mesmerized and swayed to the pulsing beat.

A swarm of monarchs descended and swirled around her—a blur of black, orange, and coral—creating an iridescent mist as if she was swaddled in the softest and lightest blanket. For a moment, resounding peace enveloped her, and she smiled. The song persisted, though, and grew louder and louder until it reached a crescendo of haunting voices. Her heart pounded. Startled, she dropped the rebozo.

The sound ceased. The mist unfurled and cleared. Glittery specks lingered in the air like suspended jewels.

"What just happened?" asked Solimar.

Lázaro twittered.

"Yes . . . peculiar." Solimar picked up the rebozo and frowned. "One side looks as if the butterfly wings are embedded in the fabric . . . and they're shimmering."

Lázaro flew closer to examine it. He grabbed a corner with his beak and shook. Nothing happened.

Solimar hurried to the water and rinsed one end of the rebozo. "It won't come off."

She glanced across the creek. "Abuela mustn't find me over here." Solimar squeezed the water from the rebozo, folded the fabric in half with the iridescence on the inside, and tied it around her waist. Carefully, she made her way back across the creek.

When she reached the opposite bank, bushes rustled nearby.

She quickly sat on a boulder as if she'd been patiently waiting there all along.

Lázaro perched on her shoulder.

She whispered, "I don't need to mention this to anyone. With any luck, the shimmering will fade quickly and no one will be the wiser."

TWO

The Almost Princess

A familiar singsong voice rang out in the forest, "Soliiimar . . . Where are you?"

"Over here, Abuela!"

Her silver-haired grandmother, Doña Ana Socorro, emerged from behind a thicket, the fringe from a purple rebozo falling to the middle of her long dress. She carried a basket already filled with slips of greenery. Although she was royalty—the mother of Queen Rosalinda, Solimar's mother—Abuela remained a dedicated herbolaria and had never given up making medicines and potions from plants and herbs.

"Abuela. Look!" Solimar pointed to the oyamel firs on the other bank.

As Abuela came closer, she admired the butterfly-covered trees and murmured, "Las mariposas. Beautiful. They are fitting ornaments for the sacred firs. And I see you have decorated yourself as well." She pointed to the elaborate crown of dahlias, then reached out and gently untangled a ribbon caught on one of the small gold hoop earrings Solimar had worn since she was a baby.

"Just call me King Solimar!"

Abuela clicked her tongue and shook her head. "A childhood fancy. Although, your hair is as short as most kings, to be sure. Solimar, please consider growing it. You're a young woman now. Do it for me? For your frail and old-fashioned grandmother."

"Abuela! You may be a little old-fashioned, but you are not frail." Solimar patted the black curls cropped close to her head. "Besides, I like it this way. If it's any longer, it becomes a tangle and makes me bad-tempered. And you know I can't endure braids or buns."

Abuela sighed. "It just doesn't look very . . . royal. You look more like a rough-and-tumble forest elf than a princess." She bent over to clip dandelion leaves.

"Where does it say what a princess must look like?" asked Solimar. "Besides, I'm not one yet. It's not official."

"I stand corrected," said Abuela. "*Almost* a princess. And it is *understood* what royalty should look like. Your birthday is only a month away, when you will become—"

"I know. I know. A princess of the world." She rolled her eyes.

"Solimar, why do you make light of it? Most girls have a quinceañera to celebrate their fifteenth."

"Not like mine!"

Abuela nodded. "True. Yours will be a little different."

"A little? The court of attendants, a party for the entire kingdom, ceremonial dances and shoes . . ."

"Solimar, this means so much to your parents, especially your mother. She has been planning this for a very long time. Be excited, if only for her."

Solimar sighed. "I will. It just seems so . . . extravagant and frivolous. I would be happy with a courtyard barbecue with an obstacle course and a climbing wall and archery games . . . instead of all the fussiness."

Abuela laughed. "Considering your courtyard is the castle grounds and your quinceañera is also your official coronation, I think the festivity warrants some pomp and pageantry. And not an athletic competition."

Lázaro chittered on a nearby branch, bobbing his head.

"After all, you will be crowned Princess Solimar Socorro Reyes Guadalupe, a descendant of Queen Isabella and King Ferdinand of Spain, who—"

Solimar repeated the litany she'd heard hundreds of times. "—who sent my father's ancestors to rule New Spain, which became the Mexican Empire, and eventually became the country of Mexico, where my father, Sebastián Reyes Joaquín met my distinguished mestiza mother, Rosalinda Socorro Guadalupe Cruz, whose great European and Indigenous family owned San Gregorio and all the land surrounding it as far as the eye could see!"

"And you, Solimar—"

Lázaro twittered as if heralding the news.

"I know! I will be crowned a princess, *never* in line to the throne and in the shadow of my brother, Prince Campeón—"

"*Constantino*," insisted Abuela. "It's time we start using his more dignified name, Prince Constantino Reyes Guadalupe."

"Abuela, it might not catch on. Everyone has called him Prince Campeón since he was a toddler. And, either way, he will be king. Which will make me . . . not king." She frowned.

"Why is that a problem? It is simply the way of the land."

"Isn't it clear? The king chooses, decides, announces, and resides above all. He anoints and dispenses and changes and commands. The king is the undisputed proclaimer and the last bastion of yes and no. And everyone obeys. But I don't want to just follow the leader. I want to have a say!"

"You will find a way," said Abuela. "Look at your mother. Your father listens to her and respects her advice, especially on matters for which she feels strongly."

"Because she happens to be married to the king! And when Campeón is ruler, it will be his spouse, not his little sister, who will have his ear."

Abuela rested on a fallen tree trunk, patting the spot next to her.

Solimar sat and sighed.

"And if you were king?" asked Abuela.

"Oh, I have so many ideas. I've been reading about a country with a round table of advisors to the king. We could do the same and it should be composed of men *and* women. I'd allow everyone in the kingdom to vote for those who sat around it. And one of the first things I'd propose is that I, and other women, could go on the expedition each year. If that was the case, I'd be packing right now."

Tomorrow morning, her father, King Sebastián, and her brother would have the enviable task of leading a caravan of men down the mountain to Puerto Rivera. There, on the outskirts of the great port town, sellers and buyers converged in an outdoor fair called El Gran Mercado. In the grandest marketplace in the twelve kingdoms, the much-coveted handiwork of the artists of San Gregorio would be displayed, peddled, and bartered.

"It isn't fair that Campeón is allowed to go and I am not."

Abuela waved a finger to dispel Solimar's notion. "It's a treacherous journey. You should be thankful you're not going. It's five days of riding a horse or leading a packed burro down steep mountain trails and across the flatlands to the port. When it's his turn to rule, your brother will need to know how to supervise this trip every year, successfully."

There was no worry that Campeón would fail. He always

lived up to his pet name: a champion in every way—of his father's pride, his mother's attention, the villagers' respect, and of every young woman's heart in the kingdom. Like everyone else, Solimar loved him, but she also wanted to go with him to El Gran Mercado.

"Abuela, why shouldn't men *and* women go, especially when in some cases, the women are better riders, the actual artisans, and more charming and knowledgeable salespeople? It makes no sense. If I was king—"

"It's how things have always been." Abuela patted Solimar on the knee. "And how things *are*. For now."

Solimar slumped and muttered, "The way of the land."

Lázaro flew to her shoulder.

"Just do me one favor," said Abuela as she sorted through the plants in her basket. "Please don't bring this up to your father again tonight. He has enough on his mind preparing for tomorrow. Wait, at least, until after the expedition to persist. Then never give up. Yes?"

Solimar smiled. "Yes."

Abuela stood and scanned the area. "Now, I've found almost everything I need to prepare the medicines for the journey. But before we head home, help me find Mentha spicata."

"Mentha what?"

"Mentha spicata. Spearmint. It's an herb I need for medicinal tea that treats headaches and stomach ailments. It usually grows in sunny patches." Abuela sighed and put her hands on her hips. "Now, where is it?"

Solimar pointed downstream and blurted, "There. Below those boulders!" She frowned. Why had she said that? Abuela lifted her skirt and hurried through tall grass and over rocks. "It's a bit of a slope. Is it safe enough?"

"No!" cried Solimar, startling Lázaro into a nearby tree. "The boulders are slick and you're going to—"

Abuela tumbled from view.

"—fall." Solimar ran to Abuela and found her sitting in a clump of greenery.

Abuela laughed. "No harm done. And look. I landed in the Mentha spicata!" She plucked several large sprigs. "I'm glad you knew this spot. Help me up, please. And let's get back to the castle. The sun is low, and there's much to be done before the send-off in the morning."

Solimar helped Abuela stand, then followed her through the forest.

As Solimar fell behind, Lázaro flew to her shoulder, and she whispered, "I've never seen that herb before. I just *knew* where it was and that she would fall. But I don't know *how* I knew. You believe me, don't you?"

Lázaro twittered before he flew after Abuela, the sun catching the silver band on his leg, which was stamped with the royal crest.

Solimar glanced back across the creek at the fir trees blanketed in monarchs. "Lucky guess . . . I guess."

THREE

Too Many Coincidences

I never grow tired of this magnificent view," whispered Abuela.

Solimar smiled and nodded. They had emerged from the forest and stopped to admire the castle bathed in the amber sunshine of late afternoon.

To the north, a jury of massive mountaintops rose above the kingdom. Somewhere within those peaks, the fountainhead of Río Diablo sent torrents of water over great falls. To the east and west, the oyamel forest blanketed the valley and the surrounding foothills. And to the south, a steep road snaked away from the village and down through rocky passes until it reached the flatlands and, somewhere far beyond, the bustling harbor town of Puerto Rivera.

As Solimar and Abuela approached the village, Lázaro flew ahead and settled in a tree near the small outdoor marketplace. Flags emblazoned with the village's emblem, a large monarch, marked each corner of the bustling town square. Familiar sounds welcomed them: Wagon wheels rumbled, fountains gurgled, and parrots squawked. A group of children ran past, laughing.

The faint smell of corn from warm tortillas pulled Solimar toward a vendor who flipped them on a comal over an outdoor fire.

"Hola, Solimar. Is it true? They have arrived?"

"Yes, Ricardo! The first wave, dazzling as ever, with many still in the sky."

"They will settle. Our forest is their chosen home. I hope they continue to honor us with their presence. They are what define us, after all."

Solimar nodded in agreement. People from the surrounding kingdoms and beyond recognized San Gregorian art by its distinctive monarch-inspired features: elaborate masquerade masks, quilted clothing, painted tin and wooden boxes, delicate embroidery, beaded brooches, and that for which they were most known: the muñecas de trapo, rag dolls with crowns of ribbons and the distinctive orange-and-black butterfly wings.

"Will we see you at the send-off tomorrow?" asked Abuela. Ricardo tipped his hat. "Yes, Doña Ana Socorro. No one would miss it. The entire village is praying for the animals to be surefooted so the caravan will reach Puerto Rivera safely. And for fair skies." He folded a tortilla in quarters and handed it to Solimar. "That is the biggest question right now. Will it rain or shine? What does our young princess-in-waiting think?"

Solimar blurted, "Intermittent and brief downpours this afternoon and tonight, a light sprinkling after midnight continuing through early morning. Partly sunny skies for the departure." Surprised at her words, she took a step back.

"Solimar! There is not a cloud in the sky," said Abuela.

"I meant . . . I . . . I *think* that's what the weather will be." Awkwardly, she smiled. "Thank you, Ricardo, for the tortilla."

"You're welcome. And let us hope you are right about the weather," he said, tipping his hat again. "Until the morning."

As they progressed through the village, Solimar took a bite of the still-warm tortilla, then tossed a piece toward Lázaro, who caught it midflight and carried it away to a rooftop.

Ahead, Solimar noticed her friend Josefina at the flower stand. She had been Solimar's mathematics tutor last year.

"Josefina!" called Solimar, hurrying toward her.

The young woman spun around, holding a flower. "Solimar! How are you?" Josefina kissed her, then nodded and curtsied to Abuela. "Doña Ana Socorro."

Solimar grabbed her hand and squeezed. "I'm fine. I miss you. My new tutor isn't nearly as fun as you were. How are you?" She grinned. "And Arturo?"

Josefina sighed. "As you probably know, he's been promoted to the king's stable master, so he's leaving with the caravan in the morning on the expedition. He asked to meet me tonight, but he was so serious and standoffish that I am worried that his feelings for me have changed. What will he tell me?"

Again, Solimar's words rushed out. "Only that he loves you and he will ask you to—"

Josefina gasped. "Stop!" Her eyes filled with hope and joy. "Solimar, are you aware of something I'm not?"

"Yes." Confused, Solimar rubbed her forehead.

Josefina hugged Solimar. "Don't say another word. I want to be surprised." Grinning, she kissed Solimar on the cheek and hurried away.

Abuela pulled Solimar close. "I can't imagine what possessed you to say such a thing. You must not play with Josefina's emotions. The heart is a very tender thing. You cannot predict Arturo's intentions. Now, what will happen if he does not propose?"

"He will." She put a hand over her mouth. The words kept slipping out!

Abuela took a step back and shook her head. "Solimar! You *must* not presume—"

Before Abuela could continue, Mónica and Vera, two of

Campeón's friends, burst from the dress shop. They curtsied to Abuela, then crowded around Solimar, politely kissing her cheeks.

"How are the king's plans for the send-off?" asked Vera. "Will it proceed as usual tomorrow?"

The words spilled. "The preparations are going accordingly, except there is one lame horse that will be left behind."

"And Prince Campeón?" asked Mónica, lowering her voice. "Is it true he will make an announcement about choosing a bride tomorrow? Or does he intend to wait until the caravan returns?"

Solimar plunged into an answer. "My brother will not make an announcement about choosing a bride tomorrow, and at this time he does not intend to return with the caravan."

Abuela stood straighter. "Please excuse my granddaughter. She is mistaken. I've heard nothing about a lame horse. The king *has* spoken to the prince about choosing a bride. And you can be sure he will return with the caravan."

The girls looked at each other, then back at Solimar.

She blushed and stared at her boots. "My apologies. I misspoke. My grandmother knows far better than I."

Mónica and Vera sighed with relief, curtsied to Abuela, linked arms, and continued on their way.

Abuela set her mouth in a straight line. "This is not like you, Solimar. I've never known you to behave this way. I hope you are not unwell."

Solimar had to make an excuse fast, or she'd find herself in bed facing one of Abuela's foul-tasting medicinals or stinky poultices.

"I'm fine, Abuela. Really. I think I was just trying to make conversation. And I'm a little tired and light-headed. Except for that bite of tortilla, I haven't eaten anything today."

"Well, no wonder you're not yourself. Come along." She walked decisively toward the end of the street and through the barbican, the two stone towers flanking the entrance to the castle grounds.

As Solimar followed, she whistled for Lázaro, who dove to her shoulder.

In front of the castle, Abuela crossed the spacious courtyard with its five-tiered fountain and reflecting pool. Instead of using the main entrance, though, she veered toward the side and headed down a winding stone path that led to the back verandas and the royal gardens.

María Batista, Solimar's closest friend, was just leaving the animals' patio with a large basket of eggs. Her auburn hair dangled in two long braids, and her cheeks were perpetually blushed, just like her mother's. Señora Batista was the castle's head chef, and María sometimes helped her in the kitchen.

Solimar rushed to give her a hug. They had grown up side by side, and even though María was almost two years younger, it made no difference to either of them.

María curtsied to Abuela. "Good afternoon, Doña Ana Socorro. With respect, I have an important request."

"María, for you anything, if I can grant it," said Abuela.

"Arturo, the stable master, would have come himself, but he's tending to a lame horse. He asked for a small bouquet from the garden." María put her hand over her heart, leaned forward, and whispered. "I shouldn't say, but it's *so* romantic. Arturo told the stable boy, who told my mother, who confided in me that he is going to propose to Josefina *tonight*. Might I cut some flowers for him?"

"Of course," said Abuela, turning to look at Solimar. "It seems my granddaughter had already heard the news as well."

She hadn't, but Solimar smiled weakly.

"María, please ask your mother to send some food and tea to Solimar's room," said Abuela. "She needs to eat and rest."

Before Solimar followed Abuela, she grabbed María's hand. "Can you be the one to bring the tea? I have something to show you."

María smiled and nodded.

As Solimar hurried through the garden after Abuela, the sun disappeared behind dark clouds. A flash of lightning lit the sky. Thunder cracked and echoed in the hills.

Lázaro screeched and shook. Solimar took him from her shoulder and cradled him in her arms, pulling the ends of the rebozo over him. "Lázaro is as frightened of thunder as Serafina."

"The poor things," said Abuela. "I hope Serafina, the old dear, is safe inside the greenhouse, and that she has her sock. Otherwise she'll be frantic."

Abuela's cat was affectionately attached to a green woolen

sock she had pulled from the laundry a week ago. When it was not in her possession, she caterwauled until it was found.

Fat raindrops splattered on the terra-cotta stones, causing Solimar and Abuela to dash beneath a balcony to avoid a downpour. While momentarily trapped, Abuela tilted her head and studied Solimar. "Curious, the weather. Another of your declarations came true. Now I am beginning to think a spell has befallen you."

Solimar shuddered and shook her head. Abuela would make her drink wormwood tea, or something equally disgusting, to break a spell. "That's not it. Just . . . lucky guesses."

Abuela raised her eyebrows. "Let's see if that's so. Solimar, will I find Serafina safe inside the greenhouse or huddled and trembling outside?"

Solimar braced for words to jump from her mouth. But they didn't. She forced a bright smile. "I have no idea!"

Abuela sighed. "Hmm. All right, then. Lucky guesses." She kissed Solimar on both cheeks. "I need to find Serafina, so off I go." She held the purple rebozo above her head and hurried away.

Solimar darted through the rain, too, and into the castle. Safe in her room, she settled Lázaro on his perch. He shook out his feathers and quickly hopped to his food tray, which had been filled with fruit, berries, and seeds.

Solimar's balcony faced west with a view of the oyamel forest. She opened the balcony doors and gazed out. The short cloudburst she'd predicted was over, and blue sky already pebbled the clouds.

How had she known about the weather? *Was* she under the influence of a spell? But if that was so, why hadn't she answered the question about Serafina?

Solimar crisscrossed the red rebozo around her, holding it snug. She wasn't cold, but she shivered anyway.

FOUR

Revelations

Solimar spread the rebozo on her bed and studied it, still wondering about what had happened in the forest.

There was a quick knock on the door, then María peeked in. "My mother sent chamomile tea and a sandwich."

"María, come and look at this!" Solimar pointed to the rebozo.

María set the tray on a small table, then turned to the rebozo. "It's beautiful! And the pattern of the wings shimmers orange. How did it get this way?"

Solimar put her hands together, pleading. "Promise not to

tell anyone. My mother or father mustn't find out, because I was someplace I wasn't supposed to be."

"Best friends *keep* secrets," said María. "Of course I won't tell."

"I crossed the creek to get a better look at the butterflies."

María put a hand over her mouth. "But the creek . . ."

"I know. It's not allowed. I just wanted to sit beneath the sacred firs for the arrival. And it was magnificent. I wish you could have been there. I was holding the rebozo out to my sides when a swarm of butterflies landed on it. That's when I heard singing." Solimar frowned. "Or at least I think I did. Then there was some sort of . . . frenzy. After it stopped, the air was all sparkly and the rebozo looked like that."

"Maybe when the butterflies landed on it, the sun somehow tinted the fabric with their images. It's so pretty. I'd wear it every day," said María. "I'd even drape it over my horse's neck in parades."

For as long as she could remember, she and María had trained together at the royal stables. Even though Solimar was accomplished, María was the best rider and jumper in the kingdom.

"María, there is something odd about it, too. When I'm wearing it and someone asks me a question . . ." She hesitated. "I seem to know the answer. I predicted the cloudburst, and a lame horse at the stables, and that Arturo was going to propose to Josefina. And no one told me any of those things ahead of time."

"Really?" María looked skeptical. "There must be a logical explanation."

Solimar picked up the rebozo and wrapped it around herself. "Help me test it. Ask me something about the future."

"That's easy. When will you and I ride down the mountain in the caravan to El Gran Mercado like we've always dreamed?"

Nothing came to Solimar. "I don't know." She thought back to the questions she'd answered earlier. They all had been about something that would happen today or tomorrow—within the next twenty-four hours. "María, ask me something about tonight's dinner. Something I couldn't possibly know."

"Let me think . . . Well, my mother had planned to make a pineapple cake for dessert, but only minutes ago she changed her mind. What will she serve instead?"

Solimar sank to the bed, puzzled. "I . . . I couldn't say."

María sat next to her and patted her hand. "It's all right. Maybe your premonitions were just coincidences. Think about it. The weather changes as quickly as our minds in San Gregorio. *Everyone* knows Arturo loves Josefina and means to propose sooner or later. And didn't we see a horse limping at the stables last week?"

Doubtful, Solimar nodded. It hadn't felt like coincidences. She tried to remember the conditions when she had blurted out the answers before. She'd been wearing the rebozo, someone had asked her a question, while she was . . . *outside*. Was that it? She had to be outside? But she'd been outside during the cloudburst when she and Abuela huddled beneath the balcony, and she couldn't answer the question about Serafina. Did the clouds or rain have anything to do with it? Could this intuition be affected by weather? As she thought back, a realization settled. Every time she'd made a prediction she'd been . . . in the sun!

"I just thought of something." She flung open the double doors and pulled María onto the now-sunny deck. "Ask me again about the dessert."

María rolled her eyes and sighed. "What will my mother serve for dessert tonight?"

"Orange flan."

María's mouth dropped open. "How did you guess?"

"I don't know. It just came to me. Ask me something else. Maybe about the expedition. Something I couldn't already know."

"Hmm. What about this? When I talked to Arturo only an hour ago, he mentioned that your father had just decided on the horse he would ride in the lead tomorrow. Which stallion will have the honor of wearing the king's colors?"

"Saturno."

María clapped. "That's amazing!"

"So you believe me, right? There's something magical about the rebozo."

María smiled and winced at the same time. "Magical? That would be a stretch of the imagination. But you definitely have a great intuition, and you're very clever at guessing . . ."

"But, I wasn't—"

"Soli, don't be silly. Like I said before, there's always a logical reason. . . ." She paced for a few seconds, then spun around and held up a finger. "You *did* see me earlier with a large basket of eggs, and the only dessert my mother could possibly make with so many eggs is a flan, of course. And orange flan is Campeón and your father's favorite. It's logical that she'd make what they love the night before they leave."

"True . . ." said Solimar.

"And your father is always talking about the horses. Perhaps you heard him mention he was considering Saturno for the lead and you just didn't remember."

"Maybe . . ."

"See, that's the case!" said María. Relieved, she laughed. "Imagine if you mentioned this to anyone else. Tongues would wag in the village. You'd be badgered and pursued. And then when people found out it was only a little common-sense clairvoyance, they'd think you irrational and foolish."

Solimar hadn't thought of that. Maybe it was better to keep whatever was happening a secret, even from María. She forced a smile. "You're right. Commonsense clairvoyance. It was a silly game. I knew you'd have the answer."

María smiled. "I better get back to the kitchen. There's so much yet to prepare before the send-off tomorrow. And my mother is barking orders at anyone who sets foot there." She hugged Solimar. Before she rushed away, María shook her head. "Whatever will my mother do tomorrow once the caravan has left?"

Solimar could not stop the words that tumbled out. "Meet with my mother to go over plans for my quinceañera, play cards with the kitchen staff, take a bubble bath, and go to bed early."

But María didn't hear. She was already gone.

Back in her bedroom, Solimar shut the balcony doors and closed the shutters. With the rebozo lying across her knees, she sipped the tea and nibbled the sandwich. "I don't believe María's explanation. Something happened to the rebozo in the forest, and now it imparts some mysterious intuition about the near future." A dark thought crossed her mind. "Lázaro, what if someone asks me a question, and the answer, which I can't seem to control, is hurtful, or sad, or foretells catastrophe?"

Lázaro hopped from his perch to the floor and tugged at one end of the fabric.

"I agree. Until I understand what has happened, I should hide it. That will solve the problem."

Solimar buried it in the back of her closet and closed the door. "End of story," she said, dusting off her hands. She sat at her dressing table and brushed her hair.

When she was finished, she found the rebozo lying across her bed. She shook a finger at Lázaro. "Did you retrieve it as a joke? This isn't funny."

Lázaro squawked in protest.

Solimar shook her head, folded the rebozo, and laid it in the bottom of a tall basket. She stuffed a blanket on top and closed the lid. "Lázaro, you need to leave it alone. Do you understand?"

He flew to her hand and attempted to cross his heart.

When she turned, she found the rebozo draped on the back of a chair.

She and Lázaro shrieked.

Lázaro spread his wings, shielding Solimar, as if the rebozo was dangerous.

"Let's not panic," said Solimar, taking deep breaths. "Let's try this one more time. . . ."

Lázaro leaped to her shoulder.

With two fingers, she gingerly picked up the rebozo and dropped it into a dresser drawer, slamming it shut. She and Lázaro stared at the drawer, waiting. When nothing happened, Solimar slowly backed away.

She sank into the chair next to the table where María had left the sandwich and tea.

When she turned to sip her tea, the rebozo was next to her plate, folded into the shape of a swan, like a giant napkin for a fancy party. Solimar jerked back, her heart pounding. The chair teetered and began to topple.

Lázaro screeched.

But as she fell, the rebozo lassoed the back of the chair

and slowly pulled it upright. Then the fabric collapsed onto the table.

Solimar and Lázaro stared at the crumpled heap.

Lázaro twittered.

"I'm not sure what happened, either," said Solimar.

She reached toward the fabric.

A small corner of the rebozo inched forward and covered her hand.

Solimar's brow furrowed. She didn't feel threatened by the rebozo, but she was confused and worried. "It insists on being near me, Lázaro. But why? I can't have it appearing everywhere I go, or I'd have to explain it. And I can't explain it because I don't know what magic this is!"

Lázaro made soft, sympathetic cheeps.

She strummed her fingers on the table. Who could she talk to about this? Abuela was already suspicious, and she would probably tell her mother and father. Campeón would never betray her confidence. She would ask him what to do.

"I suppose the safest thing is to keep it with me and to stay out of the sun." She picked up the rebozo, placed it on the end of the bed, and lay down.

Lázaro nuzzled next to her.

The rebozo fluffed itself over them.

For now, in the dim room, they rested.

FIVE

Alliances

B y the time Solimar woke, the sun had already set and she was late for dinner. She folded the rebozo so the shimmering didn't show and draped it over her shoulders.

Downstairs, she stopped in the arched doorway of the dining room. The long, carved cherrywood table blushed beneath two enormous candelabras. Queen Rosalinda, King Sebastián, and Señor Verde, the king's chief counsel, sat at one end, drinking coffee.

When her father saw her, he quickly stood, opening his arms. "Solimar! Finally."

Smiling, her mother waved her forward as well. She wore

a pink rebozo over a gray silk dress. In the candlelight, her dark skin glowed bronze, and her hair, twisted into an elaborate bun without a strand out of place, appeared blue-black. People said Queen Rosalinda's elegant feathers could not be ruffled.

King Sebastián, on the other hand, always looked a little disheveled, his wavy gray hair at odds with any style, his clothes a bit wrinkled from long days in the streets, stables, and fields—where he said a king belonged, and not shut away in the castle.

"Good evening, everyone," said Solimar.

She kissed and hugged her father and then her mother. She nodded to Señor Verde and sat down. "I'm so sorry I'm late. Mother, why didn't you send someone to wake me?"

"Abuela said you needed to rest. We've finished eating, but I'll call for a plate."

"No, thank you. Señora Batista sent a sandwich. I'll just have tea." She reached for the pot and poured herself a cup.

Señor Verde laughed. "Enough said. We are familiar with the chef's mountainous sandwiches! I have teased her time and again that I fully expect to find one of her cook's journals between the ham and cheese." He winked at Solimar.

Señor Verde was tall and thin with a mustache that turned up at the ends. He loved to make jokes, was nosy to a fault, and prided himself on knowing every detail of the kingdom. Behind his back, Solimar and Campeón called him the Shadow because he had the uncanny ability to suddenly appear at a person's side without anyone ever hearing him approach. As much as they joked about him, though, they respected his loyalty. He was their father's oldest friend and most trusted advisor.

"Where are Campeón and Abuela?" asked Solimar.

"Abuela is still preparing the medicines for the expedition," said Queen Rosalinda.

"And Campeón was not hungry," said Señor Verde. "He is upstairs and urgently wants to give you something. He said it's very important."

That was perfect. She could tell Campeón about the rebozo and ask his advice.

"I asked him what was so pressing," continued Señor Verde. "But he would not say. Now I am curious. You know me. I love tidbits of information." He slathered his bread with butter and continued. "I suspect Campeón is worried that come morning, with all the young women vying for his attention, he won't have a chance to say good-bye to you, Solimar. What do you think?"

She held her breath, waiting for an answer to jump from her mouth, but it didn't. This confirmed her idea that the magic didn't work unless she was in sunshine. She relaxed. "I can't imagine."

"He admitted to me that he's apprehensive about the expedition," said her father. "So reassure him, Solimar."

"Is he worried because of the tension with King Aveno?" asked Señor Verde.

Her father slapped the table. "King *Ávido* is more appropriate!"

"What's made you so angry?" asked Solimar. "I thought you were neighborly with him? Now you call him King Greedy?"

King Sebastián smirked. "I have always kept my distance because we're of different minds. I have tolerated him, nothing more. But I've come to understand that he's more dictator than king. In the last year, he's been cutting down trees on his land, stripping the hills, and selling the lumber. Now he's trying to buy land from all the surrounding kingdoms to do more of the same. No one wants to sell, but his bullying tactics have escalated and border on threats. He *is* greedy!"

"He's pressing your father to sell him a thousand acres of the oyamel forest," said Queen Rosalinda.

Solimar gasped. "But I made a solemn promise to protect the forest!"

Puzzled, Señor Verde asked, "To whom did you promise?"

"Um . . . myself. I promised myself to make sure the sacred firs would be safe forever." Solimar shuddered to think what would happen to the butterflies if there was no forest.

"Don't worry," said her father. "I've told him no. Yet I do not trust him. He says he is preparing an offer I cannot refuse." He smirked. "I can't imagine anything he could offer or threaten that would make me agree."

"Maybe the alliance will be the answer," said Señor Verde.

"Alliance?" asked Solimar.

Señor Verde put a finger to his lips and looked around to see if anyone was near.

King Sebastián leaned forward. "San Gregorio is by far the largest of the kingdoms he wishes to exploit. The others are looking to my lead. If he can bully *me* into selling, what chance will the smaller kingdoms have? So, on the Saturday after we arrive in Puerto Rivera, I am secretly meeting with the other rulers of the northern lands to form an alliance. If the twelve of us band together as allies, we can stand up to him as a unified group and say no, once and for all."

He pointed at Señor Verde. "As usual in my absence, I'm counting on you, my friend."

Señor Verde sat taller. "Of course. Juan Pedro, my new assistant, and I will oversee the day-to-day matters in the kingdom." He nodded to Queen Rosalinda. "With your majesty's knowledge and approval, of course."

King Sebastián frowned. "And if King Aveno makes another offer while I am gone, no matter *what* it is—"

The queen interrupted. "I will tell him that your heart cannot be changed."

"And I will repeat the same message in no uncertain terms," said Señor Verde.

"Thank you, both. Now if you will excuse me, I need to go check on the preparations for the send-off. Solimar, my love, I will see you early in the morning." Before leaving, he kissed Solimar on the forehead.

"May we turn our attention to more festive matters?" Señor

Verde looked at the queen. "How are the preparations coming for Solimar's quinceañera celebration?"

The queen smiled. "Next Tuesday—only a week from today—we will have the first fittings for Solimar and those wearing gowns. And the following week, the fittings for those wearing suits."

"Who is in your honor court, again?" asked Señor Verde.

The girls and boys in Solimar's corte de honor were her closest friends. She began to tick off fingers. "María, of course. Silvia, Estela, Irma, Belinda, Ava, Margarita, Guillermo, Mateo— Mother! You're not crying, are you?"

"It doesn't seem possible that in a matter of weeks you will turn fifteen and become a princess of the world, and officially princess of the kingdom of San Gregorio. It will be a great moment for all of us." The queen wiped her eyes with her napkin.

Señor Verde did the same. "It seems like just yesterday you were a toddler running around the castle with all your little friends, making mayhem and merriment."

Solimar rolled her eyes and quickly excused herself. But on the way out, she patted Señor Verde's shoulder and stopped to hug her mother's neck and kiss her cheek.

She hurried upstairs to find Campeón. She couldn't wait to tell him about the rebozo and ask his advice. And, like Señor Verde, she was curious, too.

What *did* Campeón want to give her?

SIX

Secrets

At the top of the grand staircase, Solimar spotted
Campeón outside on the balcony overlooking the front
courtyard and the fountain. Behind him, a few stars already
twinkled in the night sky.

Campeón had their father's wavy hair without the gray, and
black eyes, but that was where the similarities ended. He was
much taller than their father, and instead of the king's sense of
purpose, Campeón always seemed lost in his own thoughts.
He spent much of his time reading, even while he strolled
from one place to another, often bumping into things. As
usual, his head was bent over a book.

Solimar rushed to his side. "Señor Verde said you wanted to see me. And I have something to tell you."

"Soli," he said, putting an arm around her. "I'm so glad you're here. Everything will be so hectic in the morning. I want you to know . . . I'm going to miss you."

She laughed. "You'll be back before you know it. Although Father said you're worried about the expedition and that I should reassure you."

"I am a little nervous, but for more reasons than he knows. As usual, I am concerned about everyone getting down the mountain safely. We never know what we will find—rock slides, fallen logs, swarms of stinging flies that attack the horses and dogs. I wish there was a safer and faster route."

"If only we could send our goods down the river," said Solimar.

"True." He grinned. "If it wasn't for the treacherous rapids and the labyrinth of caves, that would be a great idea. Río Diablo has a reputation for chewing things up and spitting them out. You know what they say . . ."

She nodded. "Only flotsam survives the devil's river, and those who brave the caves either turn back . . ."

In a low and threatening voice, Campeón said, "Or are never heard from again."

She laughed.

"And that is why I will take a slow, tedious ride to the port on a stallion that senses I'm not a horseman and with a pack of guard dogs that ignore my commands. You know how I am around animals—inept."

"But it must be wonderful when you get to Puerto Rivera!"

Campeón smirked. "From the moment we arrive, it's chaotic. We pitch an encampment away from the crowds and the noise, for the animals' sake and our own sanity. Then we head to the marketplace to set up the large tent and unpack our goods. It's crowded and busy all day, and the night market goes until midnight. Everyone is exhausted. I have to share the royal tent with Father, who snores incessantly—all the while wishing I could sleep outside under the stars."

"It all sounds so exciting!"

"Maybe to you. I help out where I can and follow Father around like a puppy, pretending to be interested in . . . kingly-ness. When the week is over, I face another slow trek back to San Gregorio."

Solimar looped her arm through his elbow. They walked toward the end of the long balcony.

"Want to know the worst part, Soli? Once I'm home, there's no prospect of leaving again for another year."

"I didn't know you were so unhappy."

He blew out a long breath. "I want to go beyond where Río Diablo meets the ocean, sail the seven seas to ports whose names I can't yet pronounce. I want to see other countries and hear other languages. In Puerto Rivera, there's one long road that leads to the harbor. And every time I look down that road, I wonder what adventures await at the end of it."

"Campeón, why have you never said anything before, especially to Father? Surely you could take a short trip—"

"I have told him many times. And I get the same reaction that you receive when suggesting that everyone in the kingdom should have a vote. He dismisses me. The monarchy is what he was born into. It is the world he loves and knows. He's hesitant to change anything. I am the heir apparent and must ascend the throne." He scowled. "Everyone calls me Campeón, but I'm not even the champion of my own life." He leaned on the stone balustrade and gazed out over the courtyard, where the reflections of lantern lights danced on the water in the pool beneath the fountain.

Solimar had never heard her brother speak this way. Nor had it occurred to her that he might want a life different from the one that had been laid out for him. "Abuela said that you plan to choose someone to marry."

He rubbed the back of his neck, and his voice tightened. "Father wanted me to choose someone *before* we left tomorrow, but I convinced him otherwise, again. Luckily, that will give me the time I need to . . ." He hung his head.

"To choose someone?" she asked.

He turned and grabbed both of her hands. "No. Soli, remember when we were younger and every night before bedtime we played a game where you would guess what my dreams would be?"

She nodded. "I always made up the same story. That you would dream you could fly like a bird." She smiled. "As if I could tell you what to dream. What does it have to do with—"

"It's time for me to spread my wings," said Campeón. He leaned his head closer to hers. "You cannot speak a word of this to anyone, especially Mother and Father. Agreed?"

Solimar gulped at his serious expression but nodded.

"The last thing I want to do right now, or maybe *ever*, is get married." He took a deep breath. "I'm not coming back from the expedition."

"Don't be silly. You must!"

"Shh." He lowered his voice. "Please, just listen. Puerto Rivera is a port of call for the great ship *La Quinta*, which anchors in the harbor during El Gran Mercado. The last few years, I've made friends with the captain and the crew. And they're always recruiting deckhands."

"Campeón, you're not suggesting . . . ?"

He nodded, his gaze steady and his mouth set.

"No!"

"Soli, I've thought about this for a long time, so don't try to talk me out of it. It's what I *want*. I have a plan. On Friday night after everyone is asleep, I'll leave a note for Father and sneak away. I know how to slip out of camp through the forest, disguised as a stable hand without anyone noticing. I've done it many times before. And when *La Quinta* sails at dawn on Saturday morning, I'll already be on board."

"But isn't that the day of the meeting to form the alliance against King Aveno?"

"Yes." He nodded. "But Father doesn't need me. He's entirely capable. I would just be in the background anyway."

She frowned. What was wrong with Campeón? He was going to have all the power in the kingdom someday. "But why? When you are king you can do whatever you choose."

Campeón shook his head. "With the title of king comes very little freedom, and at this point in my life, the obligations and responsibilities are not true to my heart."

"But it is written . . ."

"*Where* does it say *I* must be king? Or that I must stay in this kingdom forever?"

She wrestled with her thoughts. He was right. "It's . . . it's just the way of the land."

"Precisely . . ." said Campeón. He pointed to the courtyard. "We used to play there with María when we were children. We'd spend entire afternoons making tents with blankets in our own little pretend kingdom. It was you who ruled us. We were *your* loyal subjects."

"It was just a children's game . . ."

"Was it? Or were we trying on grown-up lives?" asked Campeón. "Even then I didn't want to be king. I need to go away and discover my heart instead of accepting what people say I'm supposed to be. Haven't you ever dreamed of going somewhere other than San Gregorio?"

"To visit, yes! But I can't imagine living anywhere else. Campeón, please don't leave. What if . . . what if something happens to Father while you are gone?"

Campeón sighed. "The kingdom would pass to another prince, probably a distant cousin in Spain, until I could return. But don't worry. Father is healthy and strong. He wasn't planning on passing the crown to me for three years anyway. Even then, he'd be my advisor in all matters. Don't you see, Soli? This is my chance to explore. And who knows? Maybe I'll get it out of my system and return in a few months, feeling differently." Campeón attempted a smile.

He didn't sound as if he'd feel differently. Perplexed, Solimar shook her head. "Campeón, *who* doesn't want to be king?"

He looked into her eyes and said, "Me."

As much as Solimar loved her brother and wanted him near, she could feel his yearning to leave. She hugged him tight. "I will miss you more than you can imagine."

"Please keep my secret."

Her heart heavy, she whispered, "I promise."

"I need to meet Father at the stables. What was it you wanted to tell me?"

She'd almost forgotten. The rebozo! But it was far too complicated to explain in this moment, and now that he had such grand plans, Solimar didn't want to burden him. "Oh . . . well . . . only that the butterflies are here. The oyamel trees are covered. The forest looks beautiful. Watch for them."

He held her at arm's length. "I will. And when I see them, I'll think of you."

"Ahem!" Señor Verde stood in the balcony doorway.

They would have heard anyone else's footfalls on the marble steps of the grand staircase!

"Do you think he was eavesdropping?" whispered Campeón.

"No," she murmured. "He's too far away." Solimar took the book from his hands. Holding it up, she called, "Look, Señor Verde! Campeón gave me a volume of poetry."

"How sweet," said Señor Verde. "I suspected it was some such memento." As quickly and quietly as he'd appeared, he left.

"The Shadow," whispered Campeón.

Even though they both collapsed with laughter, Solimar blinked back tears.

SEVEN

Taking Leave

In the damp aftermath of the early morning sprinkles that Solimar had predicted yesterday, she pulled the rebozo around her and hurried to meet her mother and Señor Verde in the plaza in front of the barbican towers.

Señora Batista, María, and the castle staff followed.

The horses, donkeys, and wagons were already positioned in a parade-like order on the cobblestone street that led down through San Gregorio. Villagers crowded on either side. Children held their mothers' hands as their fathers and brothers kissed them good-bye, then the men joined the caravan, mounting their horses or taking up a donkey's rope.

King Sebastián stood in the lead, holding the reins of both his and Prince Campeón's horses. Behind him, men tightened the tie-downs on horse-drawn wagons loaded with boxes and bags stuffed with the kingdom's arts and crafts. Up and down the departure line, men checked the bulging packs on donkeys. Handlers settled the eager dogs and secured them to leashes.

Señor Verde approached the king, saying much too loudly, "King Sebastián, don't worry. San Gregorio is in good hands. I will take care of everything!"

Señora Batista whispered, "I hope this year he will not be too insufferable while the king is away."

Queen Rosalinda sighed. "He means well, and he's devoted. I think he's putting on a bit of show for his new assistant. He just tries a little too . . . enthusiastically. We will all have to be patient with him."

Solimar's eyes sifted through the crowd. Where was Campeón? He should already be next to Father. She caught sight of him on a stone bench beneath an arch of bougainvillea, sitting with Abuela. He held both of her hands and leaned his head close to hers.

Just as Solimar had predicted, a sliver of sun broke through the clouds, bathing everyone in welcomed brightness.

She scooted into the shade.

"It's time!" called King Sebastián.

Campeón hugged Abuela and then found his mother. He moved to Solimar, unintentionally pulling her into the sun.

He whispered, "I told Abuela my secret. She wants to talk to you. You're to meet her as soon as we're gone. You can trust her." He embraced Solimar one last time. "Soli, what will I dream tonight?"

Her words burst. "You will dream you are bare-chested in a crow's nest on a tall ship, disheveled and unshaven, looking toward the horizon with your arms outstretched like a bird and grinning from ear to ear."

Campeón laughed. "You're very kind to indulge me." He kissed her forehead and ran to his position in the caravan. After mounting his horse, he saluted and waved.

Solimar stepped back into the shadow of the castle, trying not to cry, but tears filled her eyes anyway.

King Sebastián raised his arm, and the caravan quieted except for the gentle snuffling and pawing of the animals. His voice rang out, strong and confident. "As your king, I ask you to pray for our safety. Wrapped in your well-wishes, we go forth to Puerto Rivera for the prosperity and future of San Gregorio! Our heart and our home! ¡Viva la mariposa!"

The crowd cheered. And the cry "San Gregorio! Our heart and our home! Long live the butterfly!" echoed through the streets.

Slowly, the caravan made its way from the castle and down the cobbled road. Family and friends fell in behind the men as they passed, following to the edge of the village, where they stopped to wave and blow kisses.

Solimar watched until the caravan disappeared. She always

felt an ache for those who were departing but never as much as she did now, thinking about her brother and how long he might be gone. "Be safe, Campeón," she whispered.

Her mother came forward, smiling. "They're off. Thank goodness for the sun. I hope it lasts. Oh, don't forget that we are having tea later today with Señora Batista and Señor Verde to talk about the quinceañera." She kissed Solimar on the cheek before heading to the castle.

Solimar found her grandmother still sitting on the bench beneath the bougainvillea arch. "Abuela, you wanted to see me?"

She patted the bench. "Sit next to me, Solimar."

Abuela took her hand. "You were right. Campeón has no intention of choosing a bride anytime soon. Nor is he planning to return with the caravan. He also told me that he just shared the secret with you last night. But you mentioned it to me earlier yesterday. I was already suspicious about your premonitions, but now I'm sure that you are under the influence of a spell. We need to discover what happened. And why. It is for your own protection."

Solimar took a deep breath. She needed . . . wanted to tell someone. If Campeón could trust Abuela with a huge secret, so could she. "I know *what* happened, and when, but I don't know why or what it means. Yesterday . . ." She bit her lip and hesitated. Would she be in trouble for crossing the creek? "Will you tell my mother?"

"Let us not concern her just yet," said Abuela.

"I crossed the creek . . ." she began. She told Abuela every detail she could remember, even that María said that all her premonitions came from the power of suggestion and common sense.

"I think you and I know it is more than that," said Abuela. "But this is not something for others to hear." She looked around to see if anyone was nearby. "Tomorrow morning, I want you to come someplace with me."

"Where?"

"I will tell you when we're on our way. Until then, it would be wise to stay inside and keep to yourself. Meet me at the bottom of the grand staircase after breakfast. I will tell your mother I am taking you with me to forage for herbs." She pointed to Solimar's wrap. "Is that the rebozo that was affected?"

Solimar nodded.

"It will need to be examined, but it will be chilly where we're headed, so wear a heavier shawl over it."

"Examined by who?"

Abuela's brow wrinkled as if she was deep in thought. Without answering, she rose and started into the garden, then she turned. "Not a word to anyone. This is a serious matter."

Solimar frowned. She had never seen Abuela so concerned, and it unsettled her. Where were they going tomorrow? And who, exactly, would examine the rebozo?

In the morning, she did as Abuela had said and found her warmest shawl. She couldn't figure out why she would need it this time of year, but she draped it around her shoulders and over the rebozo anyway.

Lázaro stirred from a nap.

"Don't get up, Lázaro. I'm going on an outing with Abuela. I'll be back soon." She kissed him on top of his head, and he sank back into the fluff of his feathers.

Abuela was already waiting at the bottom of the staircase. Even though the castle was quiet and no one was about, as soon as she saw Solimar, she held a finger over her lips to signal that they shouldn't talk. Instead of heading toward the back patio and outside, though, she pulled Solimar into the library and quickly shut the double doors.

Solimar had always loved the spacious room, where a large map in an ornate wooden frame dominated one wall. It featured all of San Gregorio and the surrounding kingdoms. She had often stood in front of it with Father as he told her the names of every road, grove, and valley. A round pedestal table with lion's-paw legs sat in the middle of the room, with heavy chairs surrounding it. Two sofas were positioned perpendicular to a stone fireplace, and bookcases lined the remaining three walls. Light streamed through yellow stained-glass windows near the ceiling, giving the entire room an amber glow.

Abuela hurried to the west wall of shelves.

"Why are we here?" asked Solimar.

"Shhh." Abuela ran her fingers along a shelf until she came

to a small book with a gold cover. She took it out, reached into the space, and pulled on something.

A section of the bookcase clicked open to reveal a passageway!

Solimar's eyes widened.

Abuela quickly replaced the book and stepped inside the tunnel. She waved for Solimar to follow and whispered, "Stay close behind me, but no talking yet. I'll explain when we're outside." She took a lantern from the wall and lit it, then pulled the bookcase door until it clicked shut. Holding the lantern in front of her, Abuela started up the passageway.

Solimar had no choice except to follow and keep quiet. The air was stale and cold. She was already grateful for the heavier shawl and hugged it around her.

"The tunnel slopes upward," whispered Abuela. "It will take only ten minutes to reach the other side, but it's a bit of a hike."

They were both breathing heavily when Abuela held the lantern higher and revealed a wooden door. "There. The way out. Stay close." Abuela pushed it open, blew out the flame, and left the lantern on a ledge in the tunnel. Then she secured the door behind them.

Abuela edged through the vines and tall bushes that hid the tunnel's entrance until they stood on a knoll north of the castle in the shadow of one of the tall mountain peaks.

Solimar pointed to a trail leading into a narrow valley. "Is that where we're going?"

Abuela nodded.

"How did you know about the tunnel?"

Abuela reached for Solimar's hand and started walking. "Many of the castles and forts built in this area had hidden passageways so that if anyone tried to attack, rob, or pillage, the family had a way to escape. My father showed me that tunnel when I was your age. I remember once there was going to be a women's embroidery circle in the library. My mother told me I couldn't attend because the women would be discussing things not appropriate for a child. I hid in the tunnel and listened from the bookcase all afternoon." She smiled. "I could hear every word they said. But there was nothing of interest to me. I was bored and stuck there until everyone left."

"Do my parents know about the tunnel?"

"I told your mother when she was about your age."

"She's never mentioned it to me," said Solimar.

Abuela shrugged. "As far as I know, I'm the only one who has used it these many years. Now, as I once made your mother promise to keep the secret, I am doing the same with you."

"You have my word. But why do you use it?"

"It's a shortcut. Instead of hiking around the castle and through the forest, I can use the tunnel, and in half the time, reach the trail's end. There is someone I often visit there."

"Who?"

"La curandera." The word trilled off Abuela's tongue as if Lázaro was singing, *coo ran der ah*.

Solimar stopped. She had heard about the curandera, the folk healer, who lived on the shadowy side of the mountain where few dared to travel unless they needed to be rid of a curse or cleansed of evil spirits. "But, she is . . . *una bruja*."

Abuela shook her head. "She is *not* a witch. Her name is Doña Flor Espinoza, and she comes from a long line of curanderas. She was my teacher, and I know her well. If she is a witch, then so am I."

"*You* cure stomachaches with peppermint tea. They say she puts spells on people, or gives them potions that make them do things they don't want to do." Solimar cringed. "Why must we go see her? You said I was already under a spell."

"Understanding why it happened will give you some control, some power over it. Besides, her enchantment is for good. Now, when we arrive, it would be polite if you do not question anything that seems . . . well, out of the ordinary or startling."

"Startling? Like . . . what?"

"Some things at Doña Flor's house are charmed. Just be . . . accepting. That's all I ask. Embrace the mystery and the peculiarities. Please?"

Solimar frowned but nodded. Charmed in what way? And, to what was she was agreeing?

EIGHT

Doña Flor Espinoza

The sun rose higher, and the world brightened, but the trail stayed in the shadow of the mountain: cold, damp, and overgrown.

The air grew misty.

Solimar heard the roar of rushing water. She moved closer to Abuela. They rounded a bend in the trail and arrived at a waterfall plunging into a wide stream that crossed in front of them. Clouded in a showery spray, a rope-and-plank bridge stretched across the churning water.

Abuela cupped her hands around her mouth and yelled,

"We must pass one at a time!" As she stepped onto the bridge, the planks swayed side to side, but Abuela was nimble and hurried across with the confidence of someone who had done it before. She waved for Solimar to join her.

Grabbing the ropes, Solimar gulped and gathered her courage. If Abuela could do it, so could she. Her heart beat faster as she plunged ahead.

When the waterfall was behind them and the mist had lifted, Solimar noticed a clearing in the distance. In the middle sat a small stone house with a red door. A thin worm of smoke curled from the chimney. On the side of the house, a rooster strutted and chickens pecked and clucked in the yard near a dilapidated coop. Three goats with bells around their necks bleated.

The door opened, and a woman walked forward to meet them. She wore a white blouse with full sleeves gathered at the cuff, a necklace made of large orange beads, and a long red skirt. Her salt-and-pepper hair dropped down her back in a long braid.

Abuela embraced her. "Doña Flor . . ." She turned to Solimar. "I would like to present my granddaughter, Solimar."

Solimar stammered. "It . . . it . . ." Was she talking to a witch?

Abuela nodded at Solimar, encouraging her to say something more.

"It is a p-pleasure to meet you."

Doña Flor embraced Solimar, kissing her on both cheeks. "Come inside. I've been expecting you, so I made hot chocolate. Let me take your heavy shawls."

Solimar frowned and whispered to Abuela, "How did she know we were coming?"

Abuela shrugged. "One never knows with Doña Flor."

Inside, the front room was dim and cluttered. A rocker made from braided tree branches sat to one side of the hearth, with two yellow chairs on the other side. A small fire danced in the fireplace. Colorful ceramic masks of the sun and the moon with hand-painted faces covered every inch of wall space.

Was it Solimar's imagination, or were the eyes on the masks following her? She pressed closer to Abuela.

A parade of muñecas de trapo wearing bright skirts and lacy blouses decorated the mantel, their hair topped with ribbon loops, and their felt monarch wings quilted with gold thread. Did one just wink at her?

"Abuela?" Solimar murmured. "What's happening here?"

"Shh." Abuela patted Solimar's shoulder to reassure her and smiled. She did not seem the least bit surprised at anything in Doña Flor's house.

Solimar looked at her grandmother as if she'd never seen her before. Why wasn't she alarmed at all the oddities? She clutched Abuela's hand, her eyes sweeping the house as they followed Doña Flor into the kitchen.

The table was crowded with baskets of grotesque roots,

pods, and withered bulbs, which looked like little goblins with gnashing teeth. Rows of jars filled with herbs lined narrow shelves. Upside-down bouquets of dried plants dangled from the ceiling. Solimar ducked to avoid a few long finger-like vines that seemed to reach for her.

Solimar's eyes darted from one unusual thing to another. She had been in Abuela's greenhouse, but it was nothing like this. Abuela grew herbs in clay pots and crushed leaves in a molcajete with a tejolote. There was far more going on in this kitchen than a simple mortar and pestle. But what?

"You're wondering why I have all these things," said Doña Flor.

Solimar's mouth dropped open. "How did you . . . ?"

Doña Flor smiled. "Your face said it all. Allow me to explain my apothecary." She went to the stove to stir the chocolate. "Aloe vera for a scrape or burn. Mesquite tea when the stomach churns. A basil steep to calm the system. Camphor poultice for rheumatism. Branches of cedar before the eyes alleviates susto, or frightful cries. Elm bark water for a clear complexion. Eucalyptus for sound digestion." She smiled at Solimar. "I could go on. There are many more verses. You see, it's how we remember the purpose for everything. And it ends with . . ."

Abuela chimed in, and together they said, "Hot chocolate to calm the soul!"

Doña Flor lifted a spoonful from the pan, blew on it, and

carefully tasted it. "It's perfect!" She ladled the warm chocolate into three cups and set them on a small tray. She took a pinch of something from a ramekin and sprinkled it on their drinks.

"What's that?" asked Solimar.

"Just a little something for relaxation," said Doña Flor. "Come along." She headed back to the front room and put the tray on the table between the chairs. "Please, sit down. Drink."

Abuela sat in one of the yellow chairs and patted the other for Solimar.

While Doña Flor lit candles around the room, Solimar leaned toward Abuela and whispered, "She put something in our chocolate. We shouldn't drink it."

Abuela rolled her eyes, picked up a cup, and sipped. "Doña Flor, the sprinkling of cayenne pepper on top is delicious."

Doña Flor lowered herself into the rocker, the chair limbs creaking. "Thank you. I find that a little cayenne makes the room and the company feel warmer—and a little friendlier."

Solimar picked up a cup and sniffed the most delectable aroma of chocolate. Feeling a little ashamed of her presumption, she smiled and took a sip, the drink sending a wave of warmth and serenity through her body.

"Solimar," said Doña Flor, "let's talk about the circumstances that brought you here today."

Any reservations Solimar had about Doña Flor seemed to

disappear. As she looked around the room, the masks looked kindly and concerned. And the dolls seemed to lean forward, as if interested in what she had to say. In the glow of the candles, with Abuela at her side and Doña Flor's kind eyes encouraging her, Solimar felt improbably . . . safe.

She took a deep breath and began. "It all started with the butterflies."

NINE

Magic

After Solimar had exhausted the story with every remembered detail, she slipped the red rebozo from her shoulders and spread it across her lap, exposing the orange shimmering.

Doña Flor leaned forward and carefully studied the fabric. After a few minutes, she nodded. "Finish your chocolate."

Solimar looked at Abuela and shrugged.

Abuela gave her a reassuring smile.

Doña Flor stood and paced with her hands pressed together and touching her lips, as if she were whispering a prayer.

She stopped and plucked a few leaves from one of the

dried bouquets hanging from the ceiling and tossed them on the fire. A crisp fragrance, like a muddle of pine and mint, filled the room. Doña Flor waved the vapors toward her and inhaled deeply.

Solimar leaned toward Abuela. "What is she doing?"

Abuela shushed her. "The strong scent of eucalyptus helps with remembering."

Doña Flor lowered herself back into the rocker and nodded. "I recall . . . although I've never seen it in my lifetime. When I was a young girl about Solimar's age, my great-grandmother, a far more powerful curandera than me, once talked about this very phenomenon. When the monarchs migrate, there are sometimes those fliers who struggle and are often too young or too weak to continue on. The monarchs are diminishing, so every butterfly counts and is needed to reproduce. If the frail can't cluster together with the others, they are vulnerable to wasps and grosbeaks who will eat them. On those occasions, the ancestral spirits of the monarchs choose a benevolent courier to protect the stragglers until they are strong enough to join the others."

Solimar put a hand on her chest. "I was chosen?"

Doña Flor nodded. "And your rebozo is the swaddle for the butterflies. You are now their protector and are inseparably connected to them."

"Inseparable. That's an understatement," said Solimar. She looked closely at the rebozo. "I can't detect a live butterfly, though. I see only the flat design and the shimmering."

"They are safely embedded," said Doña Flor. "It's part of the magic, as is the ability for you alone to bear their intuition about the near future and what lies ahead."

"This intuition," said Abuela. "Why does it work only when she is in the sun?"

"Butterflies are active in sunshine and become inactive after sunset, or when it is cloudy or shady," said Doña Flor. "So their magic only works in the sunshine. But I must warn you, Solimar. The sun has become a double-edged sword."

"Double-edged sword? I don't understand," said Solimar.

"Each day that it is sunny, you must open the rebozo to warm and strengthen those you carry. Otherwise they will never have the stamina to take leave and cluster in the trees. Yet, when you are in the sun and someone asks a question, you cannot—"

"—answer fast enough," said Solimar.

"And therein lies the burden," said Doña Flor. "For every question you answer, it drains a little of their strength. If they lose too much, they will surely die."

"But I've already accidentally answered some questions."

"More sun will return their strength. The sun is the solution and the problem," said Doña Flor.

Solimar frowned. "I must stay out of the sun when people are around, or they might ask questions of me, which would diminish the butterflies' strength and could lead to their demise."

"You've got it! Now, I advise you to tell no one about the

gift unless you trust them implicitly. Or else, within a few days there will be a line of villagers wrapped around the castle who want to know the near future. Soon, you would not be able to go outside without a crowd following and barking questions at you. And then, when the magic is drained, you'd be accused of trickery and deception. You would be disgraced."

Badgered and pursued. Irrational and foolish. That's what María had said, too. The weight of Doña Flor's words crowded the room, making it feel smaller.

"How will I know when they are strong enough to leave?" asked Solimar.

"You will know. Others will come for them."

"How long will this last?" asked Abuela.

Doña Flor pointed to the rebozo. "Until the last butterfly departs. Then, the gift of seeing the near future and the need to protect the rebozo will disappear as well."

Solimar's face brightened. "So it is only temporary. For the next few weeks, I will stay inside the castle during the day. And I'll warm the rebozo on my balcony when no one is around so the butterflies will grow stronger. If I must go out, I'll take a sombrilla to protect me from the sun. Then, when they return to the forest, I'll be back to normal again. And no one, except us, will be the wiser. It's simple."

"It's a worthy plan," said Doña Flor, though her face clouded. "But remember, nothing is ever as simple as it seems."

From the back of the house came the sounds of a crash, the goats bleating, bells clanging, and the chickens cackling.

"I've had a fox snooping around of late," said Doña Flor. "I hope it hasn't invaded my egg boxes." She hurried toward the coop.

Solimar and Abuela followed. But no eggs had been taken, and there was no fox in sight. The chickens were still agitated and flapping their wings. Doña Flor tossed a few corncobs on the ground to calm them. After much petting, the goats settled, too. Doña Flor looked around suspiciously. "Strange."

Solimar nodded. *Everything* she'd seen and heard today was strange.

They walked back into the house. As they prepared to leave, Doña Flor gave Abuela a small bag of herbs and roots.

"One more question," said Abuela. "What if someone tries to steal the rebozo? Or it falls into the wrong hands?"

"Anyone who tries to break the bond would suffer the wrath of the ancestral spirits," said Doña Flor.

Solimar gulped. "What does that mean?"

The dolls on the mantel began to chatter.

"Rage, madness, impending doom."

"It's not nice to anger the departed."

"No, sireee."

"Wrath is no picnic!"

Solimar jumped away from the mantel and pointed at the animated dolls. "They . . . they talk!"

"Of course we do," said one of the dolls.

"In many languages."

"Oh yes, quite fluent."

Doña Flor nodded. "They talk a little too much. It's very difficult to keep them quiet. But there's no reason to be afraid. Their enchantment is strong, yet they are generous souls and very helpful."

Solimar walked closer, reached out, and touched the tummy of the doll who had winked at her earlier.

It giggled!

"She likes you," said Doña Flor. "Her name is Zarita. I have a feeling"—she closed her eyes and nodded—"that you two will be great friends someday."

Adoringly, Zarita blinked and smiled at Solimar.

As Doña Flor and Abuela said their good-byes, Solimar gave Zarita a weak smile and a small wave, then stepped closer to Abuela. She was eager to get home to the safety and normalcy of the castle.

On the hike back to the tunnel, Solimar and Abuela were both quiet and caught up in their own thoughts. Solimar's mind spun with all that she'd seen and heard. When they had almost reached the passageway, Solimar asked, "Abuela, why have you never said anything about Doña Flor and all her enchantments?"

Abuela smiled. "Would you or anyone else have believed me? I am Queen Rosalinda's mother and King Sebastián's mother-in-law. If I admitted to believing in more than my herbs and teas, I would be an embarrassment to the kingdom."

Solimar shook her head. "You'd never be an embarrassment to me."

Abuela smiled and took her hand. "I'm proud of you, Solimar, for listening and not overreacting at Doña Flor's."

"Abuela, what magic do *you* possess?"

"Nothing that compares. I tried a love potion on Serafina and the stable cat, hoping to make them compatible. But I wasn't exactly successful. I put a drop in their food to make them receptive to love. Then, when they were together, I rang a bell to trigger the response. But instead of falling in love with each other, they fell in love with the first *inanimate* object they touched. In Serafina's case, it happened to be that green woolen sock she carries everywhere. And the stable cat is now smitten with a curry brush. The effect should only last a few weeks. But I'd say the recipe needs some refinement."

Solimar laughed.

Abuela chanted, "Curative lotions. Various potions. All conjured up by a healing barista. Such is the life of the herbalista."

A small voice joined in, "Wave eggs 'round the body to displace spells. Lady's slipper mash for ingrown nails. Houseleek halts a wound from bleeding. Camphor stops the hair from receding."

Solimar spun around. "Who's there?"

Abuela pointed. "Your pocket!"

Solimar peeked inside. "Zarita!"

The doll giggled.

Solimar picked her up so they were eye to eye.

Zarita flapped her felt wings and grinned.

Abuela shrugged and laughed. "Doña Flor *did* say you two would be great friends someday."

Solimar stammered, "I—I didn't think she meant today!"

TEN

Fittings and Alterations

The next morning when Solimar woke, she pulled a blanket over her head.

Any other day she would have dressed and rushed outside, even before breakfast. But after everything that happened yesterday, she was happy for the solitude and protection of the castle walls. Besides, she was determined to stick to her plan to avoid the sunshine and anyone who might accidentally ask her a question.

She stretched but sat up abruptly when she heard talking coming from her balcony. Who could be out there? She was on the second floor! Flinging the covers off, she tiptoed to the door and peeked out.

Zarita chattered. "No, I can't fly even though I have wings. I'm a doll, remember?"

Lázaro nodded and gurgled.

"Good question. I came from the house of Doña Flor Espinoza. She is the curandera."

Lázaro yelped.

"No, no. It wasn't frightening at all to live with her. She may be powerful, but she's very kind. She slipped me into Solimar's pocket to give her moral support during this unusual and challenging time. By the way, where did you come from? I don't think I've seen a resplendent quetzal around here before. Or one as big as you."

Lázaro cooed and cheeped.

"Really? You're Guatemalan? Interesting!" said Zarita.

Solimar stepped onto the balcony.

Zarita turned to her. "Láz just told me that he was a gift from another kingdom to your family on the occasion of your birth."

Surprised, Solimar looked from Lázaro to Zarita. "You understand each other?"

"You can't?" asked Zarita.

Solimar shrugged. "Well, I talk to him and he seems to know what I'm saying and I sometimes presume what he's saying back to me based on his body language, but I'm only guessing, so . . . no. Not really."

"Well, luckily I speak bird and the dialect of quetzal, among other things," said Zarita. "And by the way, he said he doesn't really care for seed pods. He's more of a fruit-and-berry guy. And avocados are his favorite."

"I'll remember that. What, exactly, did you do to him?"

Lázaro strutted and chirped as he showed off his long tail feathers, which were braided and looped with brightly colored ribbons.

"He said that he loves the look. Not for every day, of course, but for special occasions," said Zarita. She sighed, dreamy-eyed. "Like a quinceañera. Láz told me that soon your court will come to the castle to try on the gowns and the suits."

Solimar smiled. "Yes. Tuesday for those wearing gowns." Solimar didn't know who was more excited, her court or their parents. She suspected the parents. And now Zarita.

Solimar peered over the banister into the vast garden below, where the busy palace staff came and went. She sighed.

Lázaro shook his head and made a clicking sound.

Zarita nodded. "That's right. When others are around, sun is your enemy."

"I know. Don't worry," said Solimar. "I'm staying in." She stepped to a corner of the balcony where there was a splash of sun and opened the rebozo to warm it. "This is only temporary, remember? Until they're strong enough to fly away."

Lázaro and Zarita nodded.

Solimar read all morning, and after lunch, she cleaned out her closet, then, pressed for something to do, alphabetized the books in her room. That night before bed, as Zarita undid Lázaro's ribbons, Solimar said, "See how much I accomplished today? There's a benefit to staying indoors! It's not so bad."

Saturday, when her mother invited her to walk to the village, Solimar pretended she wanted to stay inside and make bread with Señor Batista. When the sun made an appearance, she stood on her balcony and held the rebozo open. It pulsed and shimmered. But nothing of consequence happened.

Sunday it stormed, and except for a stroll beneath the covered patios, Solimar and María worked on a jigsaw puzzle in the library for most of the day. That night in her room, Solimar tried to sound cheerful. "At least with the dreary weather, I didn't *mind* being stuck inside. Really. I didn't."

Zarita rolled her eyes. "Right."

Monday, the skies cleared and Solimar's enthusiasm for her plan waned. First, she had to feign a headache instead of going to the stables with María for her riding lesson. Then she had hoped to convince Señora Batista her headache was gone so she could help in the kitchen again, but the chef was on her way out—to the market with Abuela.

Even though she felt sorry for herself and out of sorts, she spent the day alone in her room. This time, though, when she stepped onto the balcony and held out the rebozo, allowing the sun to illuminate it, several large butterflies flew toward her from the forest. As they drew closer, the mysterious chanting echoed.

Others will come. It was just as Doña Flor had said.

"Are you here for them?" whispered Solimar.

As the butterflies hovered in front of her, the rebozo trembled. One butterfly, then another, followed by half a dozen emerged from the fabric, flitting around her in a joyous dance. Several landed on her face for the briefest moment, their wings brushing her cheeks before they trailed away in the sky. She had saved at least a few! Were they saying thank you? The responsibility and affection she felt for the monarchs filled her with the desire to make sure the others remained safe. "I'll protect you," she whispered.

The dress fittings for the quinceañera were tomorrow, but Solimar wasn't worried. They would be inside the castle. It would be easy enough to guard the rebozo.

The next day, Solimar put her hands on her hips and announced, "I don't need chaperones. I can go to the fitting by myself. The sewing room is *indoors*."

Lázaro squabbled.

"Láz is right," said Zarita. "You should be grateful for us. A rogue sunbeam and a question at the wrong moment— snap! Your cover would be blown. So where you go, we go. Besides, we're dying to see the dresses."

Solimar shook her head. "Zarita, I can't risk you startling

anyone. You would have to be still and quiet. And I'm not sure you're capable."

There was a knock at her door. "Solimar?"

"That's María." Solimar looked at Zarita.

Zarita flopped onto the bed and talked without moving her lips. "Stiff limbs, no talking, limp wings, vacant stare, lifeless. I got this."

María entered. "My mother asked me to bring you a tray with some toast and juice. Everyone will arrive within the hour for the fittings. I'm to remind you to bring your new shoes to try on with your gown." María smiled. "Can I see them?"

Part of the quinceañera tradition was for Solimar to enter the festivities wearing the flat shoes of a young girl. She would then sit in a chair of honor placed in the middle of the dance floor. Her father would step forward, holding an open shoe box with a pair of more elegant, high-heeled shoes. He would remove the flat shoes from Solimar's feet and slip on the others, signifying her passage from childhood to womanhood. Then Solimar and her father would dance a waltz.

After the quinceañera, she would be considered a princess of the world. And, she would also officially be crowned Princess Solimar Socorro Reyes Guadalupe of San Gregorio.

Solimar retrieved the shoe box from her closet and set it on the bed. She opened the box, pushed aside the paper, and held up the silver shoes.

"They're beautiful!" said María.

"Except I haven't learned to walk in them yet. I wobble every few steps."

"You'll practice. I can't wait for my quinceañera so I can be a princess of the world, too," said María. "Then we'll be able to go to dances together and wear longer dresses, put our hair up—well, I will at least—and have shoes with heels."

Solimar groaned. "It sounds like a lot of work. And uncomfortable." She lifted her skirt. "Besides, I prefer my hiking boots."

María laughed. "Of course you do! Soli, aren't you just a little bit excited?"

Solimar smiled. "Yes. A little. It's just so over-the-top."

"A quinceañera and a coronation? It deserves to be. Thank you for asking me to be in your court."

Solimar hugged María. "You were my first choice."

"You will be my first choice, too, when it's my turn. Oh, and one more thing," said María, "after you eat your breakfast, go straight to the sewing room for the alterations. Your grandmother will be there. Your mother will meet you as soon as she can. She said to start without her."

Solimar frowned. This wasn't like her mother. She'd been waiting for this day for months. "Why? Where is she?"

"In the library. She is meeting with Señor Verde, Juan Pedro, and King Aveno."

"King Aveno? What is *he* doing here?"

María shrugged. "He arrived this morning with an

entourage of guards. I took a tray into the room for them. It's some sort of boring meeting. I better go. I have a few things to do before the fitting. See you soon."

"Yes, soon," said Solimar. Poor Mother. She had to deal with King Aveno on today of all days. He was probably making another offer on the land. Mother and Señor Verde would tell him what Father had said—that no decision could be made at this time. And, hopefully, that would be that.

After breakfast, Solimar dressed in a camisole and underskirt with a blouse and skirt on top, then carefully draped the rebozo over her shoulders. She considered Zarita. She *had* been quiet while María was in the room. Solimar slipped the jubilant doll into her skirt pocket, beckoned Lázaro to her shoulder, and walked down several long corridors toward the sewing room.

Even before she walked through the doorway, the hum of excited conversation reached her. María rushed to Solimar and grabbed her hand. "Wait until you see! The dresses are a rainbow of colors. Mine is turquoise. Estela's is pistachio. And yours is a deep coral."

María led her to where all the gowns were displayed on dress forms, each one similar in fabric and style, but none as full or as beaded as Solimar's. Her gown had a fitted waist, a bodice covered with lace, and an enormous frothy tulle skirt with sequins embroidered in the shape of tiny butterflies. The dress reminded her of the full-bloom floribunda roses in the garden.

Solimar spotted Abuela and Señora Batista sitting in chairs on the other side of the room, near the open door to the back staircase that led to the kitchen. Solimar waved to them.

The head seamstress, Señora Vega, clapped her hands. "Each of you please stand on a platform so my assistants might help you into your gowns."

Solimar and her friends found their places.

Señora Vega removed the coral dress from its form and carried it toward Solimar, smiling. "Ready?"

Solimar stood on a platform in her underskirt and camisole, keeping the rebozo in her hand. She caught Zarita peeking from the folds of the skirt she'd draped over a chair. Solimar glared at her until she popped out of sight.

The seamstress slipped the ball gown over her head. "Let me hold your wrap, Solimar," said Señora Vega. "So we can get the full effect."

"No! I mean, I'm a little chilly." Solimar flipped the rebozo over her shoulders.

There was a large oval mirror positioned opposite Solimar. She couldn't stop looking at her reflection. Was she really seeing herself? She tried to imagine what she would look like with a tiara on her head. She slid her hands into the tulle on either side of the skirt and found what she was hoping for. "Pockets! How did you know?"

Señora Vega laughed. "I've been dressing you since you were a child. I knew exactly what you would like."

When Solimar turned around to show the others, the mothers gushed their approvals.

Solimar felt a twinge of regret that her mother was missing the fitting. What could be taking so long?

"Now, Solimar, let's try it with your heels," said Señora Vega. "So I can pin the hem."

Solimar lifted her skirt to reveal her boots. "Couldn't I just wear these?"

Arms flew up, and fingers shook.

"No!"

"It wouldn't be appropriate!"

"The wrong look altogether!"

"Heaven forbid!"

"But they're so comfortable," said Solimar.

Señora Vega raised her eyebrows. "Where are your quinceañera shoes?"

"I meant to bring them. They're in my room. I'll run and get them." Before anyone could object, she hopped from the platform and ran from the sewing room, holding up the bulbous gown so she wouldn't trip on its length.

When she reached her room, she grabbed the shoes. She knew how she would handle this. At the quinceañera, she would participate in the shoe ceremony and the dance with her father. Then she'd excuse herself and put on her comfortable boots. And no one would know the difference.

On her way back, she took the shortcut and darted

downstairs and through the kitchen, clambering up the back staircase. Just before she reached the sewing room door, piercing screams rang out from inside.

Solimar froze on the threshold, the silver shoes slipping from her grasp and rattling down the stairwell.

ELEVEN

Hostages and Spies

The sewing room erupted into mayhem.

Mothers called for their daughters. Girls cried. Footsteps scuffled. Chairs tipped over. A man's booming voice ordered, "Be quiet!"

Abuela and Señora Batista now stood with their backs to Solimar, blocking the entrance to the sewing room. Abuela glanced over her shoulder and caught sight of Solimar. Her eyes filled with alarm, and almost imperceptibly, Abuela shook her head. With a hand behind her back, she waved for Solimar to go away. Then Abuela slowly pulled the door almost completely shut.

Where was her mother? Solimar couldn't leave until she knew. She peeked around the door.

Unfamiliar guards surrounded everyone. One stepped forward and announced, "By order of King Aveno, you are all under house arrest and may not leave the castle."

Solimar sucked in her breath.

Boots clattered as an entourage of more guards pushed their way in, marching Señor Verde and her mother to the center of the room!

Juan Pedro followed. But he was walking with the guards! Wasn't he Señor Verde's assistant?

"Everyone, take a seat!" insisted Juan Pedro.

Unaccustomed to Juan Pedro giving orders, no one moved.

"Now!" yelled a guard.

Solimar clasped her hands together to stop them from shaking.

While the mothers, daughters, and seamstresses huddled together in chairs and on the fitting platforms, the distraught Señor Verde sat next to Queen Rosalinda, who put a protective arm around him.

The room hushed.

King Aveno entered, flanked by his lieutenants.

He was the antithesis of King Sebastián and looked as if he rarely came off his throne or horse. His face was round and reddish, his cheeks bulgy, and his hair slicked down with pomade. He was immaculately groomed—his white shirt starched, his pants pressed into knife pleats. Rings studded his fingers, and an enormous gold coin dangled from a lanyard around his neck.

Abuela stepped forward. "What is the meaning of this?"

King Aveno smiled and bowed. "Doña Ana Guadalupe, how nice to see an old acquaintance. Now, to the pressing circumstance. With King Sebastián gone, I could not resist this vulnerable moment to gain the advantage I needed to negotiate for the land I wish to buy."

Queen Rosalinda's face was like stone. "Holding us hostage until he agrees to sell you a thousand acres is blackmail. Not a negotiation. When he returns . . ."

"What? There will be an alliance against me?" He laughed. "One of my many spies told me all about the meeting."

Juan Pedro smiled.

"And I've already arranged for King Sebastián and the prince to be 'intercepted' on their way to the meeting. So it will be of no consequence. The other kingdoms are too small and pathetic to make a move against *me*. Rest assured, your king and prince will be escorted back here, where I feel confident the thousand acres will be handed to me in exchange for your safety. If King Sebastián cooperates, we will all go back to the way things were—two neighboring kingdoms disregarding each other and living peacefully side by side."

Señor Verde looked miserable. "I am so sorry, Queen Rosalinda. I did not know there was a traitor among us."

"Juan Pedro, you are Señor Verde's assistant!" said the queen. "This is how you repay San Gregorio? Where is your allegiance?"

He smirked. "My only allegiance is to the king who will make my life more financially fulfilling. At the moment, that is King Aveno. And don't worry, we will keep you safe and make you all comfortable. *If* you cooperate. Now, where is the young Solimar?"

"Why?" asked the queen.

"Oh, you thought this was only about the land?" said King Aveno. "*She* is actually our greatest concern. I need to ask her a few questions."

Solimar pulled away from the door. He couldn't possibly know about the magic. Could he?

"Where is she?" yelled Juan Pedro.

Señora Vega stammered, "Sh-she left, t-t-to—"

Abuela raised a finger. "It is my fault she is not here. *I* sent her to retrieve my sewing basket. I needed my little gold book that lists all the types of stitches so we might have an embroidery circle for the hem of her quinceañera dress."

Solimar frowned. Little gold book? Embroidery circle? What was Abuela talking about? Her mind raced. And then she knew. The passageway.

"And where is your sewing basket?" demanded Juan Pedro.

"I couldn't quite remember," said Abuela. "You see, my memory is not what it used to be. So I sent Solimar to check my herbarium. And I told her if it wasn't there, to try the stone bench under the bougainvillea arch in the garden. Or even possibly the animals' patio."

King Aveno gave a nod to the guards, who dispersed down the front stairs.

Solimar inched away from the door, then tiptoed down the back stairs and through the kitchen. She waited until she heard the guards outside in the garden calling to one another before she darted to the library, closing the double doors behind her. As quietly as she could, she rushed to the book-case, found the book with the gold cover, reached behind it, and pulled the lever.

The entrance to the tunnel popped open.

She replaced the book and ducked inside the passageway, pulling the bookcase toward her until it clicked in place. She put a hand over her heart, taking deep breaths to try to calm the hammering in her chest.

A few moments later, Solimar heard voices in the library and leaned her ear against the door. She recognized King Aveno and Juan Pedro. Abuela had been right. She could hear every word they said.

"Send guards house-to-house and take attendance of all the residents who remain," said King Aveno. "Tell them, and the castle staff, we will be checking on them every day and if we find anyone missing, it will bring harm to the hostages. How many do we have?"

"Queen Rosalinda and her mother, four seamstresses, Señor Verde—the conscientious fool—and seven young women and their mothers, including the castle chef. We're missing Solimar, but we will find her. Come to think of it, I haven't seen that fancy pet bird of hers, either. It never leaves her side and has a band on its leg with the royal crest."

"It will be easy to spot. Tell all the guards to keep an eye out for it. Get the chef and her staff back in the kitchen to start making meals," said King Aveno. "Do you have everyone in position in Puerto Rivera?"

"Yes, guards all over the marketplace, some in uniform, some in disguise," said Juan Pedro. "There are spies everywhere. Someone will be watching the king and the prince's every move at all times."

"Good. Now, you are *sure* about the soon-to-be princess?"

"Just as I reported," said Juan Pedro. "I was on horseback on my way to meet with you when I saw Solimar and her grandmother near the waterfall. It seemed odd they were so far from the castle, so I followed them to the house of the curandera. I stood at the window and listened until the goats started nibbling on my pants and caused me to fall."

Solimar clasped a hand over her mouth. That was what had caused the strange commotion at Doña Flor's.

Solimar heard them pacing. "Can you imagine if I could use her little gift to my advantage?" said King Aveno. "I could determine my friends from my enemies, who is weak and who is not. I would know the outcome of business negotiations ahead of time. I could change the course of the world to my benefit. The power would be endless."

"The magic is short-lived," said Juan Pedro. "And it only works when she is wearing the rebozo."

"That's why we need to capture her as soon as possible. Offer a huge reward for anyone who brings her to me. And tell *no one* about the magic. That is our little secret."

Juan Pedro chuckled. "Don't worry. As long as you pay me what I'm worth, we will get along fine. And Solimar couldn't have gone far. Before we took the hostages, we counted the remaining horses. They are all there, so she's on foot."

"She could have tried to follow the caravan," said King Aveno. "Send guards to search the roadsides all the way to the marketplace. Where else could she have gone?"

"Look at the map," said Juan Pedro. "There is no other way down the mountain and only a few places to hide, unless she went to seek help from the curandera. Wherever she is, she's trapped."

"Send riders to the old woman's house," said King Aveno. "Inspect every inch of the property. And post several guards there."

Solimar heard their footsteps fade away and the library door shut. She couldn't go back inside the castle. Her mother, Abuela, and the others would be safe for now. Her thoughts raced to her father and brother. Campeón was planning to disguise himself and board the ship the night before the meeting, which would leave Father alone the next morning and heading into a trap. Campeón would want to help. She was sure of it. How could she get word to him and Father? If only she could magically transport herself to Puerto Rivera.

Juan Pedro was right about one thing. She was going back to see Doña Flor, but she had to hurry.

She lit the lantern and made her way quickly through the passageway. When she reached the other end, she blew out the light and slipped out the door.

A loud whistle startled her, and she spun around.

Lázaro and Zarita sat on a nearby boulder.

She ran to them, hugging them tightly. "I'm so glad to see you! How did you find me?"

"When the chaos ensued, Láz scooped me up," said Zarita. "And given the clues from Abuela, we figured you'd be here sooner or later. And where you go, we go."

"You figured right. And we have to hurry," she said, tucking Zarita into her pocket. "Fly directly above me, Lázaro, and be on the lookout for guards." Gathering the hem of her dress into a giant knot, Solimar ran.

TWELVE

Escape

Solimar stumbled up the path, the dress catching on bram-
bles, but she kept running until she reached the plank
bridge at the waterfall.

Taking a giant breath, she gripped the ropes and forged
ahead as the bridge swayed. On the other side, she bent over,
putting her hands on her knees until she could catch her
breath. She looked back to make sure no one was following,
then hurried across the clearing to the stone house.

With Lázaro shadowing her, she burst through the red door
and spilled into Doña Flor's arms.

The dolls and masks prattled with concern.

"Poor child."

"What has happened?"

"Oh my, she's distraught!"

"What a poor, bedraggled mess!"

Doña Flor smoothed Solimar's hair, then led her to a chair by the hearth.

Zarita climbed to the mantel to reunite with the dolls. Lázaro perched on Solimar's shoulder, his head twitching right and left, wary of every oddity in the house.

Doña Flor shushed the room. "Solimar, what has happened?"

Between nervous gulps, Solimar told the story. "We need to somehow warn my father and brother."

"Then we haven't much time." Doña Flor paced.

The dolls and masks all began to utter their concerns.

"The poor queen trapped in the castle!"

"And the princess-to-be, the only hope!"

"But the danger!"

"So many lives at risk. What can be done?"

Doña Flor held up her hands until the room quieted again. "Solimar, there *is* a way to Puerto Rivera other than by land. And it's much quicker."

Doña Flor opened a cupboard and pulled out a garment—a short vest that tied in the front and was considerably overstuffed.

The dolls applauded.

"Of course!"

"A perfect choice!"

"Bravo!"

"What? What is a perfect choice?" asked Solimar.

"This vest is stuffed with the fluffy fibers from the seed pods of kapok trees," said Doña Flor. "When you wear it, you will be unsinkable."

"Unsinkable? But what good would that . . . ?" Solimar's eyes grew large and afraid. "Río Diablo? No!"

"It's been done before," said Doña Flor. "In a canoe. And it will only take a few days."

"Can't you just do something with magic and get a message to my father?"

Doña Flor smiled. "I wish it was so, but no. Now, on the river, you will have to scout and portage around the impassable. But you can do it."

"Portage?"

"Carry or drag the canoe overland to safe water. Your grandmother told me you're a horsewoman. If you can lift a heavy saddle onto a horse, you're strong enough to portage a small canoe. And it's the only way to get to your father in time. Now keep in mind, the vest will make you unsinkable but not unbreakable," said Doña Flor. "So use the paddle to keep the canoe away from rocks and boulders."

Solimar frowned. "So if I fall into the water, I will float, but I could be smashed to smithereens?"

"Good. You understand." Doña Flor studied Solimar up and down. "Let's get you out of that dress." She opened a drawer and pulled out a blouse and brown full-legged trousers. "Much better on the river, yes?"

Solimar stared at the clothes, then around the room at the masks and dolls, who nodded encouragement. What might happen to her family if she didn't try? Would she have a home to which she could return?

From the mantel, Zarita said, "You've got this."

"I've got this," whispered Solimar. She took the clothes and quickly changed. The trousers came to the top of her boots, which she was grateful she was still wearing, instead of her quinceañera shoes. She loosely rolled the rebozo and weaved it through the belt loops, securing it around her waist, then held open a pocket for Zarita. "Coming?"

Zarita leaped from the mantel into the pocket. "I wouldn't miss this adventure for all the ribbons in Mexico."

Solimar slipped into the vest, tying the straps so it fit snug to her chest.

Doña Flor gathered up Solimar's enormous quinceañera dress. "If the guards find this, they'll know you've been here. We need to hide it. Time to go. Follow me." She headed toward the door.

The dolls and masks said their good-byes.

"¡Buena suerte!"

"Safe passage!"

"¡Adiós!"

"Bon voyage!"

Solimar followed Doña Flor across the clearing, looking over her shoulder to make sure the guards weren't near.

Lázaro, the goats, and the chickens paraded after her.

At the edge of the woods, Doña Flor stopped and pointed downhill. "Hike to the river, then downstream to a hut. You can't miss it. The canoe is inside. Launch from there. The river will be calm for most of the day, but later this afternoon it will run swift. When the current brings you to a great flat pool as spacious as a lake, you must paddle with all your might to the left bank to avoid the first waterfall."

Solimar's eyes crinkled with worry. "Waterfall? You didn't say anything about—"

"There are two, the second worse than the first. Tonight, tether to the bank and sleep in the canoe. Tomorrow morning, portage around the waterfall. But before you get back in the canoe, walk to a high spot where you can scout the next stretch of water."

"Scout for what?"

"Obstacles in the river so you'll know where they are and can paddle around them."

A cold, perspiry panic washed over Solimar. She clenched and unclenched her fists. "But . . . but how will I know what to do?"

"The river will make the choice known. Now, listen carefully. This is *most important*. Tomorrow, you will arrive at the confluence of two rivers. The one on the left leads you to the labyrinth of caves. *That* is the way you must go. The other would take you to El Salto de los Ángeles."

"Leap of Angels? What is that?"

Doña Flor shuddered. "It's the second waterfall, and you

do not want to go there. The water leaps over the falls and crashes so far below and with such force that the spray rises up in a wild froth resembling angel wings."

Solimar gulped and tried to steady her breathing. "Avoid the waterfalls. Stay to the left. And to the left. I'll remember. But the labyrinth? People go in and are never heard from again. How will I know which way to go?"

Doña Flor took both of Solimar's hands in hers. "When you come to an impasse or face uncertainty, there is only one thing to do. Trust your instincts. You are stronger than you know. And you have something special deep inside you. The butterflies recognized it, or they wouldn't have trusted you with their magic. Use it. I know you can do this. I *feel* it."

Zarita whispered. "I feel it, too."

Lázaro tweeted.

Uncertainty overwhelmed her, but Solimar nodded anyway.

In the distance, horses whinnied.

"The guards," whispered Doña Flor. She put the dress into Solimar's arms. "Hide this in the canoe hut." She turned to the goats and chickens. "Run back, my lovelies, and startle the horses."

The chickens and goats turned and fled toward the house. Within moments, there was a loud commotion of bleating and cackling and neighing.

Quickly, Solimar hugged Doña Flor. "Thank you, with all my heart," she said, and darted into the woods.

THIRTEEN

Caught

Solimar hurried down the slope toward the water's edge and followed the river downstream. On the narrow bank, she high-stepped over rocks and wove around boulders until she reached a small wooden hut on a flat and sandy beach. Solimar pulled the door open.

The canoe was smaller than Solimar expected. Two paddles lay in the bottom and a long rope dangled from the bow. Coils of old rope hung on the walls, as well as a few weathered baskets and rusty tools. Doña Flor had said to hide the dress. But where? Solimar walked to the back corner, where she found a canvas tarp.

She held up the dress and admired the lacework and sequins. She hadn't wanted any of the extravagance or fussiness of a quinceañera, but now she felt a pang as she realized she might not ever have one.

Fighting back tears, she quickly folded the gown and hid it under the tarp.

Solimar dragged the canoe from its shelter, closed the shed, and then pushed the small boat into the water. Like a sentinel, Lázaro perched on the edge of the bow. Zarita sat next to him, unusually quiet.

After Solimar looked around one last time for anyone who might have followed, she climbed inside and paddled downstream, reliving everything that had happened in the castle. Was she doing the right thing? Could she get to the port in time? Even so, what would happen to the kingdom if she couldn't find her brother and father? She took deep breaths, trying to calm the jumble of questions and worries.

The day wore on. There wasn't a wisp of wind. The water mirrored the sky so that it looked as if she were paddling through clouds. The current rested before the divergence of two small tributaries. She stopped. Doña Flor hadn't said anything about a split. And this wasn't the great flat pool as spacious as a lake. Which way should she go?

All the things she'd heard about the river crept into her thoughts. She whispered, "Only flotsam survives." Fear gripped her. What lay ahead? Her hands trembled.

Lázaro hopped on her shoulder and made short encouraging tweets.

Zarita murmured, "Trust your—".

"—instincts. I know what Doña Flor said. But what if it's not true? What if I'm not stronger than I know? What if my instincts are incorrect? Which way should I go?"

A butterfly darted in front of her. She looked up. A flight of monarchs trailed above. A small swarm broke off and flittered around her. On her waist, the rebozo stirred.

Solimar unleashed the fabric and held it out, fingertip to fingertip, letting the sun infuse it. She heard the chorus again—mystical and ancient and with such harmony that her arms prickled and tears filled her eyes. A clutch of monarchs lifted from the rebozo, their wings beating in time to the rhythmic song, and trailed after the swarm toward the waterway on the right.

Before she could lower the rebozo, the canoe began to move, the fabric acting as a sail. What force moved them forward? The canoe glided to the right, following the monarchs' path.

Solimar draped the rebozo over her shoulders and picked up the paddle. "Thank you. Fly safe," she whispered.

After she'd been on the river for most of the afternoon, the currents grew stronger and the canoe traveled faster. Ahead, Solimar saw white water and small rapids. The canoe bounced over them.

"Whee!" squealed Zarita. "That was fun!"

The rapids propelled them into an expanse of water—the

lake that Doña Flor had mentioned! Ahead, the massive pool disappeared over a drop-off. Somewhere below, water rumbled.

Lázaro frantically waved Solimar toward the left.

"I'm *trying!* But the undertow is strong!" She stroked harder, but the canoe began to spin. Was there a whirlpool beneath the water? As much as she tried to paddle backward, Solimar could not prevent the canoe from being drawn toward the edge. The roar of the waterfall grew louder.

Lázaro took flight, circled, and dived back toward Solimar, flapping his wings and screeching a warning.

Zarita disappeared into Solimar's pocket.

The canoe lurched forward. Fear overwhelmed her.

Unsinkable but not unbreakable.

She gripped the sides of the canoe tightly, her knuckles whitening.

She saw a net ahead! It stretched across the river from bank to bank, the top rope taut, the bottom web dangling like a curtain. Was it some sort of weir to catch fish? She didn't care. If she could grab hold, it would be her salvation.

The canoe drew closer to the net. On the other side, the water tumbled and sprayed. As the front of the canoe slid beneath the net, she grabbed the top rope, scrambling for a foothold in the webbing. Cowbells tied on the rope clanged.

The canoe plummeted over the falls. Her heart sank as she watched it tumble downriver and split apart on the rocks below. The rope was wet and slippery. Solimar didn't know how long she could hold on. She moved one hand and then the other. One foot and then the other. She gripped the rope as tightly as she could, swaying above the water. One hand slipped. She screamed and grabbed the net again, clinging to it.

The net began to move toward the far bank.

Someone was pulling her across the river!

Inch by inch, the net moved closer to the shore. When she was over solid ground beneath the trees, she let go.

Lázaro dove to her side.

Slowly, she sat up. "We made it, Lázaro! I'm not sure how . . ." She stared at the wide net that stretched across the entire river and back again, winding around what looked like giant spools on each bank.

A boy jumped in front of her and pumped his fists in the air. "Yes! It worked! I saved someone!" He grinned, proud of himself.

He looked a few years older than Solimar. His long, dark hair was tied back with string. His trousers had been cut off at the knees and were held up by a rope. A pair of binoculars dangled over a shirt that, although unstained, had the unmistakable dinginess of river water. Solimar had seen huaraches before—many villagers in San Gregorio wore the leather sandals—but none like these this boy wore, with thick rubber soles and heavy fabric straps crisscrossing his instep.

As he helped her up, he said, "I'm forgetting my manners. I'm Rigoberto Ayala Bernal, Berto for short. And you are?"

"I'm . . . I'm Solimar. And this is Lázaro." Her pocket

wiggled as Zarita tried to climb out, but Solimar gently pushed her back inside. It was too soon to introduce Zarita. "What is that contraption?"

"I call it the Confiscator. I wove a net waist-high and attached the top to a long rope, which is threaded onto the groove of old wagon wheels on each bank, parallel to the ground. When they rotate, the entire net moves in a giant loop. I got the idea after watching people in my village string clotheslines between buildings on a pulley. See . . . the wagon wheels are connected to gears that I can crank from this side. I've watched any number of things go over the falls. And it's not a pretty sight. I've caught fish, of course, and once a lame duck, and another time a baby beaver. I returned it to its mother. But I've never caught a person before." He smiled at her.

"It's ingenious," said Solimar. "It . . . *you* saved my life, and I'm grateful. Maybe someday I, or my family, can repay you. Right now, though, I'm in desperate need of a canoe. Mine went over the falls. By any chance, do you have one?"

"I have a way to get down the river, yes. But—"

"I can promise that if you help me get to Puerto Rivera, my father will be extremely grateful."

Berto hesitated and shook his head. "I don't . . ."

"Please? So much depends upon it. Will you at least hear me out?"

Berto shrugged and smiled. "Okay. I'll listen, once we're safe." He swept an arm toward the branches above them.

She looked up. "Why must we talk wherever it is that you're pointing?"

"Well, the sun will set within the hour, and dusk is when the coyotes, mountain lions, and skunks come to drink at the river."

Lázaro flew into the tree and disappeared.

Solimar nodded. "You're right. We should move. But . . . how?"

Almost completely camouflaged against a tree trunk, several ropes dangled. Berto pulled one—and above them, the canopy of leaves began to move.

FOURTEEN

Houseboat in the Canopy

The branches above them separated to reveal a platform built around the massive tree and fenced with bamboo and river reeds.

"It's shaped like the hull of a boat," said Solimar.

Berto laughed. "Precisely. The trunk is its mast; the canopy of leaves, its sails; and farther up . . . well, you'll see."

Berto pulled another rope.

A ladder descended to the ground.

He scaled the rungs and climbed through the opening to a deck above. He peeked down at her. "Welcome aboard."

As Solimar quickly climbed up, one of the rungs cracked beneath her boot.

"Don't worry. I can fix that!" he called, holding out a hand and helping her to the small landing. Berto hoisted the ropes, which lifted the ladder.

Within the leafy cover they were completely sheltered, except for a few dappled patches of sunlight, which Solimar carefully avoided. A row of shelves—long wood planks separated by large rocks—hugged the railing and held a collection of books, their covers and pages weathered and wrinkled.

"This is the library," he said. "I fished the books from the river. They're a little worse for their journey, but once I dry them, the pages are wrinkled but entirely readable. And there's more." He pointed upward. A narrow wood staircase spiraled around the thick trunk and disappeared.

"Where does it lead?" she asked.

"Come on!"

She followed him up to the cradle of the tree to a much larger landing. One corner was covered with a thatched roof and partially enclosed with a reed partition. Solimar peeked around it.

"Sleeping quarters," said Berto, nodding to a hammock and a mattress that looked as if it had been made from blankets stuffed with feathers.

The rest of the platform was a shady open-air galley, with a large barrel for a table and two smaller ones for chairs. An upturned crate held a stack of plates, and a tower of teacups, most of them chipped. A metal tub sat on top of a large rock.

"What is this?" she asked, pointing to two ropes strung taut in the kitchen.

"Watch." He pulled down on one of the ropes, hand over hand, until a small bucket appeared, spilling water into the tub.

"You put all this together from what you've found in the river?"

"Yes. Thanks to the Confiscator. The cowbells let me know when something is caught. You'd be surprised at what comes my way. The river just keeps on giving."

She pointed to more stairs spiraling around the tree. "Where do they go?"

"I'll show you after you change into some dry clothes." He handed her a pair of baggy pants and a shirt, much like the ones he was wearing, and sent her behind the partition.

"Your clothes and life vest should be dry by morning," he called.

As Solimar changed, a soggy Zarita crawled from the pocket. "How much longer must I be quiet?"

"I can't spring you on him all at once," said Solimar. "There's a lot for him to consider first. Stay here? Or hop in?" She pulled open the pocket of the pants.

Zarita's wings drooped, but she climbed in.

Solimar grabbed the rebozo, even though it was still damp,

and draped it over her shoulders with the shimmering on the underside. It would dry soon enough.

She followed Berto up the staircase. The higher they climbed, the sparser the leaves, but with the sun dropping behind them, the neighboring trees cast them in shadow. At the top, Solimar found herself standing in a large wooden crow's nest, like the one in Campeón's dream.

"A lookout," said Solimar.

Berto nodded. "I call it the Crown."

"I wish my brother could see this. He would love it."

"You have a brother?"

She nodded, feeling a tug on her heart. "He's leaving on a long sea journey soon, as . . . a deckhand." She turned toward the river, her eyes sweeping over the panorama: the steep canyon walls, the river, and the waterfall slipping over a lip of rocks and crashing far below, more dangerous than she could have imagined.

"Look this way," said Berto, pointing in the opposite direction toward a brown and barren horizon. "See the opening between those two mountains in the distance? That leads to my home, Valle Granada. And true to its name, it is a valley of hundreds of acres of pomegranates. Unfortunately, it lies between two monarchies but neither claims us, both rulers stubbornly insisting the responsibility lies with the other." He shrugged. "I guess you could say Valle Granada is a kingdom-less land, with no protector or allegiance. My family is still there—my mother and sisters and . . . all the others."

"Why are you here, so far away from home?"

"Until now, the pomegranate has meant prosperity for all the farmers who live there. But the natural springs and the wells are drying up. At this rate, in a few years there won't be enough water for crops. I came here, next to the falls where there is water to spare, so I could create a way to channel some of it to my village. I'm working on a few ideas."

She walked slowly around the platform until she came to a narrow opening with a wooden slide. "And this?"

"The fast way down. I'm a bit of a flume-ologist."

"A what?"

"I build flumes—chutes and slides and such. I made this one by snagging barrels from the river, cutting them in half lengthwise, opening the top and the bottom, laying them end to end, and then sealing the joints. Or I capture long lengths of wood, soak them in water so that they're bendable, and curve them over a form. My . . . my father taught me. But catching barrels or wood in the net is difficult and doesn't happen very often."

"So that's how you're trying to get water to your village. You want to divert it from the river with flumes."

"Yes," said Berto. "With flumes and canals I could move a lot of water a long way. On this end, I'd construct a gate to control the flow. Then, near Valle Granada, I'd build a reservoir, releasing the water as needed. All I need is supplies and manpower."

"What kind of supplies?"

"Donkeys here at the base to run a wheel that lifts the water from the river. Lumber or barrels for the flumes . . . I know. It seems unbelievable to think I could accomplish such a thing. But I have to try." Berto's face clouded and he gazed past her. "The fate of my entire family and my home is in my hands."

Tears filled her eyes. She swiped at them. "Mine too."

For a few moments, they said nothing, each lost in their own worries.

Berto cleared his throat. "You said you needed help?"

Solimar took a deep breath and gave him a crooked smile. She nodded toward the slide. "Maybe we should go down first."

He sat at the top of the chute and pushed off, his voice fading as he yelled, "See you at the bottom!"

Zarita popped her head from the pocket. "It's stuffy in here."

"I know it's hard to wait. Just a little longer," said Solimar. "Now, enjoy the ride!" She sat on the ledge and pushed off just the same. The slide curved in a wide arc and deposited her on the deck near the shady kitchen. She jumped up, laughing. "That's brilliant!"

FIFTEEN

The Appeal

With Lázaro on her shoulder, Solimar sat at the make-shift table on a small barrel across from Berto.

"I have a confession. I am the soon-to-be-crowned Princess Solimar of San Gregorio. My father is King Sebastián and my mother is Queen Rosalinda."

Berto scratched the side of his head. "Uh-huh. That doesn't make sense. Didn't you say your brother was a deckhand?"

Solimar nodded. "But he is also Prince Constantino, otherwise known as Prince Campeón. He's running away from home to join a ship because he doesn't want to be king anytime soon, or possibly ever."

Berto looked skeptical. "Okay . . . *That's* not something you hear every day."

"No, it's not," agreed Solimar. "Even so, I desperately need to intercept him before he gets on that ship."

"Why?" asked Berto.

Solimar barely took a breath telling him all about King Aveno and his wish to buy a thousand acres and exploit them, the hostages, and how her father would be walking into a trap when he left for the secret meeting. "And there's more." She hesitated and considered whether to tell him the rest. Yet she sensed she could trust Berto. Besides, what choice did she have? "King Aveno wants to capture me, too, because of a newly bestowed gift."

He tilted his head, confused. "Gift? What kind of gift?"

"Before I say, you must promise to be . . . accepting."

He rolled his eyes. "I promise."

Solimar took a deep breath and told him about the monarchs, the sword of light in the oyamel forest, the magic, and the rebozo.

Berto stared at her with a blank look. "Are you sure you didn't bump your head when you dropped from the net? Do you feel dizzy or light-headed? Are you seeing double?"

"No!" she insisted. "And it's all true!"

Berto gave her a weak smile and shook his head. "You must admit this all sounds a little far-fetched."

Solimar called for Lázaro, who landed on the table in front

of Berto and held up his leg to present the band with the royal crest.

Berto put out his hands. "He's your pet and has an identification band. That doesn't prove anything."

Solimar untied the rebozo from her waist, unrolled the fabric, and flipped it onto the table to reveal the shimmering.

He pointed at it. "Unusual . . . and pretty. And this, *supposedly*, gives you the ability to . . ."

Solimar nodded. "See the near future."

Berto stood and ran his fingers through his hair. "Before the sun goes down, I need to check a net I strung across a stream. It's where I usually catch dinner. And I don't think we should be heading down the river anytime soon. You seem a little delirious. Maybe you should rest. Take a few days."

"Delirious? Rest? I don't have *time* to take a few days!" said Solimar. "You don't seem to grasp the . . . the . . ."

Berto spread his hands and held them in front of his chest. "I'll be right back, and then we can sort out what's *true* and what's *imaginary*." He headed toward the ladder.

"I can prove it!" said Solimar.

Berto turned around.

She stood and stepped away from the table and into a small patch of sunlight, then flipped the rebozo over her shoulders. "Ask me what you will find in your net."

He raised his eyebrows. "Sure. I'll play along. What have I caught in my net?"

Her words flew. "Two mullets, a bass, a basket, a broken spoon, and an almost-drowned rat tangled in fishing line, a green duck feather. And a blue glass marble."

He chuckled, gave a dismissive wave, and climbed down the ladder.

When he was on the ground, Lázaro flew after him, whistling.

Solimar propped an elbow on the table, resting her chin in her cupped palm. With the other hand, she drummed her fingers on the uneven wood.

Zarita peeked from the pocket. "I suppose it had to be done to prove your point."

Solimar nodded. "We need him."

It wasn't long before Berto was back, his face sober. He held up a line with three fish attached and placed a damp and battered basket on the table.

Solimar peered inside. She lifted out a broken spoon, a green duck feather, and a blue glass marble.

Lázaro whistled a victorious fanfare.

"I untangled the rat and set it free, and I'll fry the mullets and bass for dinner." He sat and stared at Solimar. For a moment, he didn't say anything. "I . . . I . . . caught a *princess* in the Confiscator?"

"Almost a princess. It's not official for a few weeks."

"Still . . . royalty."

Zarita popped out from Solimar's pocket. "Yes! Now we're getting somewhere!"

Startled, Berto jerked back and toppled off the barrel.
Solimar jumped up to help him. "Are you all right? She
didn't mean to startle you. I know it's a lot to take in. I should
have eased you into the charmed doll thing." Her eyes pleaded
for him to understand. "Berto, meet Zarita."

Zarita curtsied. "Don't be alarmed. I'm kind and helpful
and mostly unassuming."

He righted the barrel and sat down again, his eyes darting
from Zarita to Solimar. "Almost a princess. Charmed doll.
Magic rebozo. Anything I should know about Lázaro?"

"Oh no. Don't worry, he's not magical, exactly," said
Solimar. "Although he can communicate perfectly with
Zarita."

"Of course he can," said Berto.

Zarita put a hand on her chest. "You see, I speak the quetzal
dialect. And squirrel, coyote, dog, and enough cat to get by."
She leaped to the table and faced Berto. "You *must* help.
Please?"

"If we're successful," said Solimar, "I promise I'll do everything in my power to get you supplies and labor for your
flumes and reservoir."

Berto chewed on his bottom lip, thinking. Then he put his
arms out to the side, palms up, raising one hand and lowering
the other, as if weighing his choices. "Help the princess-to-be
save San Gregorio and have a grateful king as my ally and
benefactor . . ." He shifted his hands. "Or refuse, and know
that I contributed to the destruction of a beautiful forest and

the demise of not only the monarch butterfly but possibly an entire kingdom." He looked into the canopy. "Hmm. *Of course* I will help you! I can't say no to the chance to save my family and yours."

Solimar clasped her hands together and smiled. "Thank you! The sooner we leave, the better."

"First thing in the morning, then. I dock on the other side of the falls, where the white water levels out. You'll need to help paddle."

Solimar nodded. "I can do that."

As Berto cooked the fish, Solimar set the table. "How long will it take to reach the port?" she asked. "I need to arrive by Friday night to warn my brother and father."

"Based on what I know, two full days on the river. So tomorrow and Thursday. Then it's a day hike to town. So with any luck, we *should* reach the marketplace sometime on Friday." He looked at her bare feet. "You'll need river sandals."

"I like my boots."

Berto shook his head. "They're heavy, and once they fill with water, they'll be like anchors. The soles are too slick, and they take forever to dry, making it difficult to go from land to water and back again. Trust me. You need light all-terrain shoes for sloshing in water, hiking, and rock-climbing. Or you'll slow us down."

After they ate, Berto put a piece of thick leather on the deck and pointed to it. She stood on it as he traced around her feet with a pencil. Then he carefully cut foot beds to match the outlines. With an awl and a hammer, he punched dimples into the rubber soles. He tore three long strips from a cotton blanket, and then began to tightly braid them.

"When the straps are done, I'll push the ends of the fabric through the holes, knot them, and crisscross them over the top. You'll be able to tie them snug to your feet. They will be comfortable and practical, if not fashionable," said Berto. "I bet the last time you had a pair of new shoes, they weren't like these."

"No," she murmured. "They were very different." The silver quinceañera shoes were neither comfortable nor practical, yet her heart tugged as she imagined how proud her father would have been to change her flat shoes of childhood for those of a woman, and how excited her mother would have been to see her in her gown and tiara. She smiled. She would be happy to wear the silver shoes now, wobbly or not . . . if she could make the recent turn of events go away.

The sun set and the air cooled. Berto handed her a blanket. "It's early to bed and early to rise on the river. I'm afraid the hammock isn't fit for royalty. But it will have to do." He went back to working on the sandals.

Solimar climbed into the hammock, put the blanket over her legs, and draped the rebozo over her chest. Lázaro and Zarita nestled at her feet. The rebozo felt heavier than usual. Was it the burden she carried—the fear that she would not be able to warn her father in time and change the destiny of her kingdom?

She squeezed her eyes tight and tried not to cry.

SIXTEEN

River Craft

After Solimar woke and changed back into her clothes, she tied on the vest, situated Zarita in a pocket, and hurried from the sleeping quarters but found herself alone.

Her new river sandals sat on the table. Berto must have been up for hours last night, finishing them. Solimar put them on, tied the straps, and walked back and forth. They *were* comfortable.

She stepped into a sunny patch on the deck and held out the rebozo for a well-deserved warming to replace any strength that might have been lost last night. Then she carefully wrapped it around her waist again.

"Coming down . . ." Berto slid onto the kitchen platform, holding binoculars and wearing a life vest of his own. "I was checking the river. Our first run looks relatively calm."

She modeled the sandals. "Thank you."

"You're welcome." He shook his head. "A soon-to-be princess is wearing the shoes *I* made for her . . . I never saw *that* coming."

"No time to be starstruck," said Zarita.

"Yes, we should get going," said Solimar.

Berto stuffed a few blankets into an oilskin tote, rolling the top and tying it snug. "This is our dry bag." He slung it over his shoulder and swept an arm toward the ladder. "Your river chariot awaits."

They hiked up a steep trail behind the tree house, across a ridge, and down again toward the river to circumvent the waterfall. Ahead was a flat stretch of the river. "That's the shallows, where we'll put in," said Berto.

Solimar set Zarita on a boulder. "Where is the canoe?"

"I guess I should have explained. See, I *had* a canoe, but the hungry river chomped it in half and . . . well, I lost it. So I built a small . . ." He hesitated.

"Boat?" she asked.

Berto winced. "You *could* call it a boat."

Solimar stopped. "Wait. You *said* . . ."

"I said I had a way down the river." He walked to a pile of branches near the water and pulled them aside.

Solimar sputtered with disbelief. "It's . . . it's . . . a raft!"

It was as long and wide as a canoe. Narrow logs were the base, and it was topped with short ones that had been laid perpendicular and lashed together. In the center, battered window shutters were strapped down. Two upturned crates served as benches on the front and back. Used paddles lay the length of the sides, stacked snugly beneath ropes.

Proudly, Berto said, "I snagged everything in the Confiscator, and I named it *La Magdalena*."

"But it doesn't even have sides or a railing!"

Berto looked as if his feelings were hurt. "It's perfectly capable. And I've already taken it on short jaunts. There is no reason it shouldn't make it farther. Besides . . ." He shrugged. "It's our only option. And look!" From behind a tree, he pulled a long, narrow bundle of tightly woven fronds.

"What is it?" she asked.

He hopped onto the raft and positioned it in a hollow piece of bamboo affixed to the crate near the bow. He propped open a giant leafy umbrella. "A sunshade. So you won't have to worry about me accidentally asking you questions for which I don't need to know the potentially terrifying answers, like whether or not we're going to survive. Or what danger lurks around the next bend, which would be *so* handy to know. But I'll forgo the advantage with respect to the lives of the butterflies and your wishes. See? All the conveniences."

The umbrella collapsed over Berto. From underneath came his muffled voice. "I can fix that."

Solimar's heart sank. Her voice quivered. "How . . . how

are we supposed to portage around dangerous sections of the river?"

"We don't," said Berto, crawling from beneath the umbrella. "The raft is much too heavy. But I've scouted the river many times, and I have run every rapid all the way to Devil's Teeth. That is, when I had my canoe."

"Devil's Teeth? Is that where the hungry river chomped it in half?"

"Well . . . yes. But it's only called that because when the water is low the gigantic boulders look like a mouthful of jagged teeth."

Solimar's eyes widened.

"But don't worry, the water level is high now, so it might not be as threatening."

Solimar gulped. "*Might* not be."

"We'll scout ahead and take it one rapid at a time. After Devil's Teeth, we're home free and only have to navigate the caves. . . . You're not hyperventilating, are you?"

Zarita nodded. "She's having a moment."

Solimar walked in a circle, taking deep breaths, her arms flailing up and down. She bent over, put her hands on her knees, and dropped her head forward. When she straightened, she laughed and cried at the same time. "The plan is ludicrous! Nothing *survives* Río Diablo! Not even your canoe! We'll soon be stranded, and I will never intercept my father in time. And the labyrinth of caves? I've heard the stories. It's a maze! People go in and never come out."

"Not *all* people. I know someone who almost made it through the entire labyrinth. And he gave me very specific directions."

She stopped. "Did you write them down? Or did you make a map?"

"No. And no." With a finger, he tapped his temple. "But I memorized them."

"You memorized them?"

Berto nodded. "A hard right. A flash of light. Track your voice. A boat-less choice. Drop of doom. A sapphire room. Bright of day leads the way."

"Those aren't directions! They're . . . They're . . ." Solimar pointed at Berto. "Wait! How far did this person get, *exactly*?"

Berto shrugged. "To the 'track your voice' part. Then he was forced to turn around and go back. But *only* because the weather outside turned bad, making conditions inside the caves too dangerous—high water and flooding. So far, we have good weather, so I can almost guarantee . . ."

"He *almost* made it? You can *almost* guarantee?" Frustration gripped Solimar. She clenched her fists.

Lázaro flew to Zarita, plucked her up, and dropped her into Solimar's arms.

"Okay. Pep talk time," said Zarita. "Look at me. He seems sincere, and more importantly, he's all we've got. And that life vest you're wearing that keeps you afloat and makes you unsinkable . . . well, it's . . . it's a metaphor! Because unsinkable means a lot of different things besides *not* drowning. It means that you can't be kept down. It means you keep trying, no matter what. And that you're un-cowardly and unwavering and unstoppable! Besides, Doña Flor said you have instincts. Remember?"

Lázaro squawked and nodded.

Solimar squeezed her eyes tight, wiping the tears away, and took a deep breath.

Was Zarita right?

She looked from the raft to Berto. "The person who gave you the 'directions' for the labyrinth . . . was he honest and trustworthy?"

Berto gazed downriver and nodded. "I never doubted him for a moment. He knew the river like the back of his hand. It was my father. He . . . he died five years ago."

Solimar's bottom lip quivered. She straightened her shoulders and slowly nodded. "Then let's do this."

SEVENTEEN

Rapids

After Berto repaired the umbrella and secured the dry bag to the raft, he pushed off into the shallows. "All aboard!"

Solimar sloshed through the water and climbed on, grateful to see that *La Magdalena* floated. She sat on a crate beneath the umbrella, Zarita perched above her in the struts, and Lázaro, ever-vigilant, roosted on the bow, such as it was.

Berto handed Solimar a paddle. "Everyone ready?"

She was not the least bit ready but nodded anyway.

He stood behind the umbrella with one long paddle and raked through the water like a gondolier, moving them toward the center of the river and carefully maneuvering around boulders and sandbars. "Okay, river lesson number one," he said. "Never, *ever* go on the river without a life vest." Solimar patted hers.

Zarita whispered to Lázaro, "I'm feeling a tad underdressed."

"Lesson number two. If you go overboard, cross your arms over your chest, point your legs downstream with your toes up and out of the water. That way you can push off of rocks and debris instead of crashing into them. If I'm on the raft, look at me, and I'll point to either the raft or to the shore. If I point to shore, work your way to the bank and climb out and wait there until I can get to you. If I point to the raft, stroke toward me, and I'll pull you on board."

"Got it," said Solimar.

"River lesson number three. Follow my commands. If I order *left* or *right*, dig in on that side. If I yell *high side*, rush to the edge of the raft that is elevated. If I say *stop*, bring your paddle into the raft. And *back* means . . ."

"Let me guess. Stroke backward?"

"It sounds easier than it really is," said Berto. As they drifted downstream, he watched the water. With the paddle, he carefully pushed off the rocks and logs that threatened to bump the raft.

"Did your father teach you to navigate the river?" asked Solimar.

Berto nodded and smiled. "We used to come here together, to study the waterfalls and currents and how the water behaved. He talked to anyone who lived or fished on the river, especially the older ones. That's how he came to know the directions for the caves. See, he wanted to figure out a way to move water from the river to Valle Granada. *And* find an easy way to transport crates of pomegranates downriver to Puerto Rivera to sell."

"I've always wondered how to do the same for San Gregorio," said Solimar. "The problem is not only getting the goods downriver, but then getting the people back up to the village. If only there was some sort of transport system."

Berto nodded. "That's what my father thought, too." He cleared his throat. "People in Valle Granada made fun of him, saying his ideas were wild illusions. But he believed he could do it. He was the one who taught me all about building things and engineering. The flumes were his idea. He never lived to see his hopes and dreams come true. He left my mother, my four younger sisters, and me to carry on."

"I'm sorry," said Solimar.

Berto sat on a crate, stroking on one side of the raft and then the other. "There are riffles coming up—shallow but fast-moving water. Get ready for small bumps and splashes."

Solimar held on. The continuous riffles sent the raft speeding over a long stretch of water . . . until they slowed again. The water quieted, and they barely moved. It was as if the river took a breath and held it.

"Why did you name the raft *La Magdalena*?"

"Magdalena is my mother's name," said Berto, smiling.

"She loves Valle Granada. All her memories are there. Mine too. When the springs and wells began to dry up, I went to the adjoining kingdoms to ask for help with my father's ideas. But the king's advisors laughed at me. In their eyes, the land in Valle Granada is a lost cause. And maybe it is. But I must try. My mother never lost faith in my father's dreams or in my ability to see them through. So . . . *La Magdalena*."

His story tugged at Solimar's heart. "It is a beautiful name."

"What about your dreams, Almost-Princess Solimar?" asked Berto.

She blew out a long breath. "Well, before all of this happened, I wanted to change things in my kingdom. I have ideas about forming a council of men and women who advise the king, and allowing everyone in the kingdom to vote."

"That's a very big dream."

"Yes, and now it might be for nothing if I . . . we . . . can't save San Gregorio."

Berto murmured, "Dreams are never for nothing." He moved them forward, the only sound the slurp of the paddle as it cut through the water.

The river exhaled, and more riffles sent the raft flying forward again, filling Solimar with optimism. It was the same all morning—moments in the fast-moving water, followed by an absorbing stillness. Still, if they kept up this pace, they'd make it to the port safely and with plenty of time.

In the afternoon, Berto guided the raft to the bank and tied it to a sprawling tree. In front of them was a steep hill, now in the shadow of the canyon walls. "We need to hike up there and scout what is beyond."

Solimar scrambled after him to an outlook, surprised at how easily she could climb from the water and then across boulders in her river sandals.

Berto raised the binoculars to his eyes and studied Río Diablo. Then he handed the binoculars to Solimar.

Below them, the river ran through a long, straight canyon bordered by rock cliffs.

"When we reach the canyon, there will be a few small riffles, then a whirlpool. We'll have to dig in hard to avoid it."

Solimar slowly moved the binoculars downstream. "It looks calm after that."

"The river is deceiving. Never trust it. Notice the top of the water and how it ripples toward the right and splashes against the cliff. The current is strong there. We don't want to get pulled against that rock face. Once past the whirlpool, we need to paddle to the left, or the current will pull us over. Look farther downstream. What do you see?"

Solimar shifted the binoculars. "Calm water and then one rapid and a short break, then two, three . . ."

"Keep looking. It's five rapids in a row," said Berto. "I call it the String of Pearls."

"Do we try to avoid them, too?"

"Nope. We run right down the middle of them and face the waves head-on. It's going to be a bumpy ride. I made it through with the canoe. We should be fine."

She handed him the binoculars. "Should be?"

"Just follow my orders. This next run will test your mettle on the river. And I'll see just how worthy my crew is."

As she followed Berto back to the raft, Solimar straightened her shoulders. "You don't have to worry about me. I'm stronger than you think. Just tell me what to do, and I'll do it."

"Fair enough," said Berto.

When they reached the raft, they climbed back on. Berto took the umbrella from its holder and began strapping it to the raft.

"Wait. What are you doing?" asked Solimar.

"I have to take it down to run the rapids. Otherwise, we'll lose it. It's the only way."

Feeling exposed and vulnerable, Solimar tensed. There would be no way to stop herself from answering if Berto asked a question. "Please remember not . . ."

Berto raised a hand to stop her. "I got it. I promise."

"Cross your heart!" said Zarita.

He swiped his finger in an X across his chest.

As soon as they reached the middle of the river, Solimar felt the pull of the current. The water ran flat and fast, and the raft sped down the canyon. Soon, the riffles were upon them.

"Right! Right!" yelled Berto.

Solimar dug into the water with the paddle. The draw toward the whirlpool was strong, and it was far bigger than she'd expected. The threat of being swirled about and spit out made her strain harder on the paddle.

"Stop!" yelled Berto.

She pulled the paddle into the raft. Berto positioned the raft in the center of the river. The water quieted. Ahead, the first rapid of the String of Pearls loomed.

Berto dug in with the paddle. "Hold on!"

Solimar gripped the ropes between the logs, her heart pounding.

Lázaro screeched and took flight.

Zarita took the bow position and held on as if she were riding a bucking horse, squealing with delight.

The raft rolled into a well and smacked into white water. Then it dipped again, and another wave crashed over them. As they sped ahead toward more churning water, Solimar braced herself and closed her eyes. They barreled through the spray, and the raft rocked wildly. She thought they would surely capsize, but they came out on the other side of the roiling water, unscathed.

"Just two more to go!" yelled Berto.

Solimar clutched the ropes and gulped down her fear, knowing that each lurch forward brought her closer to her father and Campeón and that tomorrow she could be safe in Puerto Rivera.

Once they made it through the rapids, Berto grinned and nodded. "Not bad, Solimar."

She tried to look confident, but her smile was weak and her insides were still reeling from the ride.

Berto unstrapped the umbrella and propped it open above

her. Then he settled on a crate and dragged the paddle through the water. Zarita leaped to the grip, riding it like a seesaw. Lázaro circled, then landed on Solimar's shoulder.

The rest of the afternoon, Berto moved them past canyon after canyon on smooth water. After the frenzy of the rapids, Solimar was grateful for the calm. She dragged her hand in the river and stared into the clear water at a fish swimming near the surface. "Señora Batista would cook you if she could."

"Who is Señora Batista?" asked Berto.

"She is the castle chef and the mother of my best friend, María." Solimar smiled as she told Berto all about María. "I hope everyone is safe. They're all hostages now with my mother and grandmother; they must be so frightened and worried."

"They're lucky you escaped," said Berto. "And had the foresight to run to the curandera. You're their hope."

When the sun dipped behind the rock cliffs, Berto docked the raft and tied it to a boulder at the edge of the riverbank, where they made camp. In the deep shade of the canyon walls, the air cooled. Solimar untied the rebozo from her waist and draped it over her shoulders.

Berto opened the dry bag and pulled out the blankets. "Early tomorrow morning we scout and run Devil's Teeth."

Zarita chimed in. "We can do it. Obstacles make life more interesting."

"Thank you, Zarita, for the vote of confidence," said Berto. "I *am* more experienced now. And, Solimar, with your help paddling, there's no stopping us. We just need to make it through the gate, the narrow passageway entrance to the next stretch of rapids. Then after we make it past Devil's Teeth, we head to the mouth of the caves and the labyrinth." He smiled halfheartedly and shrugged. "Simple, right?"

Solimar murmured. "Right." But she couldn't forget what Doña Flor had said about nothing being as simple as it seems.

EIGHTEEN

Devil's Teeth

After a fitful night rolled in a blanket on top of a bed of leaves, Solimar woke at dawn, slipped on her sandals, took Berto's binoculars, and tiptoed away from where he was sleeping near the bank of the river.

As she hiked to the top of the steep hill behind them, she wrapped the rebozo around her to ward off the crisp morning air.

Lázaro flew after her, tree to tree.

Zarita poked her head out of Solimar's pocket. "Where are we going?"

"Shh," Solimar whispered. "I want to see what we're facing on the river and give the rebozo some sun."

At the top, she lifted the binoculars and looked downriver where they would travel today. Huge boulders shouldered together across the river except for a small passageway between them—the gate. In the river beyond, the tips of rocks protruded from gnashing white water. No wonder it was called Devil's Teeth! At the far end of the canyon, a wide expanse of water chopped and roiled—the great confluence of the two rivers. Farther out, one river branched to the left toward the maw of a giant cave. The other flowed right and disappeared into a cloud of mist—the Leap of Angels.

It looked ominous. Solimar took a deep breath and shuddered.

The sky grew brighter, and the sun peeked over a mountain. Solimar unfurled the rebozo and held it out to her sides, slowly turning. She felt the rebozo pulse and heard the chanting of the chorus.

Butterflies appeared above her, hovering.

As several monarchs detached from the fabric and fluttered to nearby wildflowers and milkweed, she whispered, "Your escorts await above." They flitted back to lightly brush Solimar's face before they took to the skies with the others. She studied the rebozo and the remaining patches of shimmer. How many more days before they were all gone, along with her power to see the near future?

Solimar rolled the rebozo, loosely weaving it through the trouser belt loops again and giving it a protective pat. She lifted the binoculars to follow the butterflies as they trailed upriver toward yesterday's path and the String of Pearls.

She froze.

Her breathing quickened.

Two canoes were staked to the bank. Inside one of them, she saw the unmistakable fluff of her coral gown and, on top of it, the boots she'd left in Berto's tree house. Nearby, four guards slept in bedrolls.

The blood drained from her face.

She ran down the hill and roused Berto. "Wake up! We have to leave now!"

He sat up, groggy. "What?"

"Guards on the bank. Upriver. Four of them. With canoes. They tracked me from Doña Flor's to your tree house, and then to here!" Solimar tugged on his arm. "Once they're in the water, they'll catch up to us in minutes!"

Lázaro squawked.

Zarita climbed onto Berto's chest. "Imminent danger," she said. "It's go-time."

"Okay. Okay. Everyone take a breath. Solimar, we have to scout the rapids first."

"I already did! Two huge boulders at the gate. Beyond, water to the top of the rocks. Only tips showing. At the far end of the run is the tunnel to the caves. Everything between looks as if the devil himself is gargling." Her eyes pleaded. "We have to hurry! They're likely still asleep, but they'll wake soon. Early to rise on the river, remember?"

Berto looked toward the hill, as if weighing a quick run to the top to scout the river himself. He turned and locked eyes with Solimar. "Only the tips of the rocks are showing?"

"Yes! We need to leave now!"

Lázaro flew in circles, squealing a warning.

"Please?" cried Solimar.

Berto nodded, then quickly put on his sandals.

They ran to the raft.

Berto stuffed his binoculars into the dry bag and secured it to the boat. He pushed off the rocks toward the middle of the river. "After Devil's Teeth, paddle hard through the chop to the left, toward the entrance to the caves."

She nodded.

Quickly, they sped down a long stretch of calm water. After they rounded the bend in the river, the boulders that marked the entrance to Devil's Teeth loomed in front of them.

They edged through the gate and dropped into a whirlpool.

Solimar and Berto paddled hard until they pulled out of the swirling water only to drop again, bouncing through wild water and heading toward a giant rock formation smack in the middle of the river.

"Back!" yelled Berto.

Solimar back-paddled as hard as she could, but the current

was fierce and propelled them straight toward a sloping rock midstream. The raft slid up the face.

"High side!"

She scrambled to the high edge of the raft, which was now suspended and threatening to flip over.

Zarita slid into the water, jetting downstream.

Lázaro flew after her.

With the paddle, Berto pushed off, and *La Magdalena* shot around the rock into a rushing torrent of white water.

Solimar lay down and gripped the straps on the shutters. The raft jolted forward, scraped over rocks, and dropped into swirling pools. She screamed, but her voice was swallowed by the roar of the water. She hung on.

As the raft rocked wildly, side to side, Berto slipped and fell into the river.

"Berto!" she screamed.

"Don't let gooo . . ." yelled Berto, his voice fading behind her.

Water crashed over *La Magdalena*. It remained buoyant but began to spin in the angry river. Solimar tightened her grip on the straps. "Don't let go. Don't let go," she repeated.

Ahead, the confluence spread before her. She bounced through the wide breadth of churning water but couldn't maneuver the raft to the left. In the distance on the right, the winglike spray from El Salto de Los Ángeles loomed.

The raft ricocheted off one boulder, then another, thudding

and creaking. Solimar's mind raced with visions of the logs splintering apart and her falling to a watery death.

A river swell lifted *La Magdalena*, and Solimar leaned as far to the left as she could, hoping to divert it. The wave shot the raft toward the bank. Solimar closed her eyes and braced for the impact. The bump almost threw her off. Trembling, she sat up to find *La Magdalena* lodged in a sandbar near the entrance to the caves.

Heart pounding, she scrambled to the edge of the raft and jumped into the shallow water. After tugging the raft over the sandbar, and just far enough into the tunnel that it couldn't be seen from the river, she tied it to a rock.

Stumbling back to the opening, she looked upstream, searching. She cupped her hands over her mouth and yelled, "Berto! Zarita! Lázaro!" When there was no answer, panic gripped her. Had they gone past her and over the falls? She called again and again, her voice desperate as she ran upstream along the narrow bank. She stopped. Had she heard something? Or was it just the rushing water? She shaded her eyes to search the river.

Lázaro appeared above her, whistling, flapping his wings, and gesturing toward the river. "Lázaro! Did they . . . are they . . . ?"

"Land, ho!" Berto, buoyed by his life jacket, floated toward her, leaning back, toes up, pushing off rocks, just like he'd instructed her earlier. As he drifted closer, he raised one arm. He held Zarita in his hand!

Relieved, Solimar ran into the water and dragged Berto ashore. "Are you all right?"

Wobbly, he sat up. "I think so. Just a few hundred bruises."

"Lázaro and Berto are my heroes," said Zarita. "I fell in and was drenched through. I sank like a rock. It was green and murky and toady at the bottom. Then this hand seemed to come from nowhere—"

"Lázaro pointed the way," said Berto. "And she was only in a foot of clear water, practically on the surface. I could easily see those bright loopy things on her head, so of course I scooped her up."

"My ribbons," said Zarita. "Another reason to always wear them. And from now on, I'll need my own personal floatation device."

Berto smiled. "I think we can arrange that." He tried to stand but quickly dropped to his knees.

Solimar pulled one of his arms across her shoulders and gripped his waist. "Come on. Let's get into the caves before the guards catch up to us."

As they stumbled toward the entrance, Berto looked around the beach. "*La Magdalena*? Did she make it?"

"She's just inside. The dry bag is still attached, but the crates are smashed, save one, and the lashings came undone, so we lost the umbrella and all but one paddle. But if we tighten the loose ropes . . ." She shrugged.

Berto sighed and smiled. "I can fix that."

NINETEEN

The Labyrinth of Caves

Solimar waded in knee-deep water, farther and farther into the caves. With a long rope, she pulled *La Magdalena* behind her.

Berto sat in the middle of the raft, steering with the paddle to keep them away from the walls. Lázaro leaned out and over the bow, as still as a figurehead, watching for danger.

Zarita hadn't left Berto's shadow since he'd saved her from the river. She was pressed to his side and now sported the life jacket he'd made from a bandanna and tufts of kapok from his own vest.

The light from the outside world still illuminated the long tunnel, its rock walls curving in and out like the deep folds of draperies. The water was a chameleon, changing from turquoise to blue to green.

"The water is so clear," said Solimar. "Like a crystal. I can see every grain of sand on the bottom."

Berto nodded. "Not much action inside the caves to muddy the waters."

As the tunnel widened, the water grew deeper. Solimar hoisted herself onto the raft. Lázaro settled on her shoulder.

Slowly, Berto paddled across the vast chamber.

Stalagmites rose from the cave floor, tapering like candles. Stalactites hung from the ceiling. The dripstones and spires met in some spots, creating twisted columns of mineral deposits. Where water had continually rushed down the walls and over rocks, minerals had built up, forming flowstones the color of cream.

"They look like waterfalls frozen in mid-descent," said Berto.

"Or the petrified fringe of a rebozo," said Solimar.

Berto stopped the raft in front of two tunnels, each veering in opposite directions.

Berto took a deep breath. "The first turn. A hard right."

Distant shouts echoed. "Hello! We know you're in there. Turn back! There's no way out! We're guarding the mouth. Call out and we'll help you!"

"Guards at the entrance," whispered Berto.

"It's a trick," murmured Solimar. "They won't help us. We can't turn back."

Berto nodded. "Wouldn't consider it. With any luck, they'll be too afraid to follow." He held a finger to his lips. "Shh. Until we get farther away. Sound carries far."

He pivoted *La Magdalena* toward the tunnel on the right. As they drifted forward, the light faded. Ominous shadows danced on the stone walls. Wind droned through the hollow passageway.

Berto kept his voice low and soft. "The wind is a good sign. And it's blowing in our face, which means it's coming from somewhere outside."

The raft scraped against something underwater and stopped.

"What happened?" asked Solimar.

"We're stuck on a submerged ledge." Berto pushed off the walls until they were clear. The raft crawled forward.

"Can't we go any faster?" whispered Solimar.

"Too many boulders beneath. I can't see where they are."

Their progress slowed. When the raft lodged on another rock, it screeched and rasped as if it might split apart.

The guards' voices reverberated in the chambers. "You're in danger! Turn around now! Call out and we'll save you."

Solimar scoffed. "They'll say anything to capture us."

"Their voices do not sound sincere," whispered Zarita.

Berto pushed off the rock. Another loud creak echoed, but the guards stopped calling to them. Were they following?

The water deepened, and they floated forward until they came to a second divide in the labyrinth. Berto stopped the raft as they considered the two shadowy tunnels. "A hard right, then look for a flash of light," said Berto.

They sat and stared into one tunnel, then the other. Solimar saw a brightening. Then darkness again. She pointed to the left. Under her breath she said, "I think I saw something."

Berto leaned forward. "Where?"

Had she imagined it? She looked into the same opening and saw a flash, like lightening. "Yes, *this* way," she insisted.

La Magdalena glided into the blackness.

The dark pressed in upon them. Solimar could not see her hand in front of her face. The raft bumped against the rock walls.

Lázaro peeped nervously and pressed against Solimar, trembling.

"In case anybody is wondering," said Zarita, "I'm officially frightened."

"Shh. It's okay," whispered Solimar, hoping it was true. Was Berto's father right about the directions? A hard right. A flash of light . . . What if he wasn't?

Ahead, like a beacon in a dark sea, intermittent light flickered.

"I see it." Berto stroked forward with purpose.

Slowly, shadows and dim light appeared again. The wind calmed.

Berto pointed up. "Look."

Far above, a flock of small birds flitted near a tiny gap in the rock ceiling, revealing a speck of blue sky.

"We're going the right way," whispered Berto.

"Thanks to your father," said Solimar.

Berto smiled. "So far, so good."

One chamber led to another. The morning wore on. They heard nothing more from the guards but were still skittish. Every sound was amplified in the caves and startled them— water dripping, the wind whooshing, a pebble falling and splashing into the water.

Time became as fluid as the river. How long had they been inside the labyrinth? Solimar wasn't sure.

They passed through more narrow passageways until they sat in a cavern facing three dark tunnels. From a crack in the rocks far above, a blade of sun pierced the water.

"Follow your voice," said Berto. "This is where my father had to turn around and go back." He took a deep breath. "We can't call out. The sound will travel. The guards will think we're yelling for help, and an echo might lead them straight to us."

Solimar closed her eyes. *You have something special deep inside of you. The butterflies recognized it, or they wouldn't have trusted you with their magic. Use it.* "Move me into the sunbeam and ask me about the tunnels."

Berto locked eyes with her. "Are you sure?"

"Yes. But ask nothing more."

Berto maneuvered the raft until Solimar was positioned beneath the stream of light.

She nodded to Berto.

Berto took a deep breath. "Solimar, where will these three tunnels lead us?"

The words raced. "The tunnel on the right is navigable, but there is no through passage. The water is stagnant and the air is foul-smelling. The one in the middle has a rock ceiling that eventually becomes so low that the only way to pass is by swimming beneath it, underwater. The tunnel on the left leads to a long corridor and a bat-filled chamber."

"Bat-filled," whispered Berto. "They would need a way in and out. That's the one."

Solimar closed her eyes for a moment and said a silent thank-you to the butterflies, along with a promise of sunshine.

Eager, Berto dragged the paddle and entered the tunnel, carefully maneuvering around jutting rocks. They inched forward.

Lázaro moaned and chattered.

"He wants to know if we are there yet," said Zarita. "He feels as if we've been in these caves *forever*. He wants to know what day this is. And he's hungry."

"I feel the same, Lázaro," said Berto. "But it's still the same day."

"It must be late afternoon by now," said Solimar.

"There!" Zarita pointed to an arched opening ahead. "Now we're making progress!"

Berto paddled the raft into a large, dim chamber surrounded by boulders and rock formations. Above, thousands of Mexican free-tailed bats clung to the walls. Water trickled down the rock faces.

"It's a dead end. There are no tunnels or corridors that I can see," said Berto. "So how do the bats get outside?"

As he moved the raft slowly around the entire perimeter, Solimar untied the dry bag, retrieved the binoculars, and scanned the room. There was a natural progression of boulders that led to a plateau above them. "Move toward the rocks so I can reach them."

Berto edged the raft close enough for her to climb off and wade to the low boulders. "What are you thinking?"

She tossed him the binoculars, put her hands on her hips, and gave a nod toward the ceiling.

He held them to his eyes. "The way out is *up*?"

She nodded. "It makes sense."

"I'll hide the raft the best I can. If the guards are ever brave enough to venture this far, hopefully they'll turn around and go back if they think there's no way out." He tucked the binoculars beneath his vest. "Guess we'll have to say good-bye to *La Magdalena* for the time being." He patted the raft.

"We'll come back for her. I promise," said Solimar.

After Berto pulled the raft into an alcove, Solimar led the way. At the top, they sidled around an opening in the rock wall into a short tunnel. Before they emerged on the other side, cool air hit them.

They stepped out onto a ledge and found themselves in a massive, cathedral-like room. Threads of daylight filtered from somewhere above.

"How high up are we?" asked Solimar.

"At least ten stories," said Berto.

"Look," said Solimar, pointing to a natural rockslide slick with water and curving down and away to somewhere far below. "It's smooth as glass."

"Thousands of years of water will do that," he said. "It's a natural flume."

"Berto, that's it. A boat-less choice."

Lázaro waved his wings and made an emphatic guttural sound.

"In case you didn't get that," said Zarita, "he said no. Absolutely not. It's out of the question. Don't even think about it."

"We have no other option," said Berto. "Besides, I don't want to spend the night in here. So it's either down the slide or go back the way we came and run into the guards." He grabbed Solimar's hands. "Everything has been exactly as my father said."

Solimar set her mouth and nodded.

Lázaro walked to the edge of the slide and looked down the chute. He backed away, clacking and squawking.

"We know it's against your better judgment," said Zarita. "But if we fall, you have wings and can fly. And I'm a cloth doll wearing a cushy flotation device. We need to go first and try out the chute to make sure it's not dangerous." She turned to Solimar and Berto. "If it's safe, we'll . . . whistle! If it's *not*, Lázaro will fly back to alert you."

Lázaro looked toward the slide and groaned.

"Come on. Let's turn worry into excitement!" said Zarita.

Sitting side by side, they disappeared over the ledge. Zarita squealed, her voice fading away, "This is fuuun. . . ."

Solimar and Berto leaned forward and listened.

Minutes passed.

"What could have happened to them?" asked Berto. He blew out a long breath. "What if Lázaro doesn't return and we hear nothing?"

"We'll hear from them," said Solimar. "I feel it."

Water trickled.

Wings fluttered nearby.

A bat screeched.

Two distinctive and familiar whistles echoed through the chamber.

"Finally!" said Solimar.

Berto laughed. "That's our cue!"

Solimar sat at the opening. Berto sat right behind her, with his legs straddling hers, and wrapped his arms around her waist. "Cross your arms over your chest, lean back against me, and point your feet forward. If we start going too fast, press your feet toward the sides of the chute to help slow us down. Got it?"

She took a deep breath and nodded.

He pushed off and Solimar leaned back. Air whooshed around them. The flume twisted and turned, but the smooth rock sides kept them contained. They slid faster and faster.

Berto whooped, but Solimar was too scared to utter a word. She wanted it to be over and to know that they were all safe.

They flew into a dark tunnel. The speed and fear took her breath away! She pressed her feet outward to slow down, but it wasn't enough. They slid up one side of the flume and then the other, almost flipping over. They were traveling too fast!

"I can't see!" she yelled. Panic smothered her.

Berto held her tighter until they passed into a cavern as bright and blue as a cloudless sky.

The flume curved, and she saw what was coming—a long slide into a steep drop to the water far below.

Berto yelled, "We can't hit the water together. You first!" He shoved her forward. "Lie down!"

She leaned back as far as she could and jetted down the chute. Her stomach turned. Her heart raced.

Solimar squeezed her eyes closed, too frightened to even scream . . . and the world fell away.

TWENTY

Light of Day

Solimar plummeted into a deep lagoon.

Underwater, she pushed off the sandy bottom to catapult herself upward. When she broke through the water and bobbed on the surface, Lázaro and Zarita cheered from the narrow shore.

Somewhere behind her, Berto yelled, "Incoming!"

Solimar dove out of the way.

Berto splashed down and popped up, spewing a stream of water. "Everyone okay? Everyone good? All arms and legs accounted for?" He scanned the grotto. "Whoa . . . look at this place."

The cavern was an iridescent jewel. The water, sand, and the rock walls glimmered aquamarine. The shadows—dark azure and indigo.

"A sapphire room . . ." he murmured.

"And look," said Solimar, pointing to the far end of the cavern, where an arched passageway led to the outside world. The incoming light created a narrow runway to the middle of the lagoon. "Bright of day. We made it. Think of what this means . . . a throughway to the port!"

Even though Berto was already wet, Solimar could see tears in his eyes. He nodded. "It could work. Put the goods on a boat, light and map the caves. Then figure out a way to get the goods to the top of the cathedral room. Maybe with a track and crank system, then longer flumes that zigzag in a gradual descent . . . but it *can* be done." Berto brushed at his face. "My father was right!" He smiled. "I knew it."

They swam to the sand and removed their life vests.

Lázaro flew ahead.

Solimar helped Zarita out of the tiny one Berto had made, then slipped the doll into her pocket. As she traipsed alongside Berto toward the opening, Solimar's clothes clung to her and dripped. She wrung out the hem of her trousers and blouse the best she could and patted the rebozo wrapped around her waist.

Lázaro let out a panicked whistle.

"I'll tell her," said Zarita. "Solimar, sunshine ahead."

At the entrance, Solimar stopped at the edge of the shade. She grabbed Berto's arm. "Lázaro is right. The sun is still up.

We could encounter anyone along the way. If I'm in the sun, and if someone simply asks me who I am or what brings me here, I'll blurt out everything."

Lázaro squawked from a nearby banana tree in the midst of its enormous leaves.

Berto ran to the tree, stood on tiptoes to reach one of the lower stalks, and tugged on it until it broke off. He brought it to Solimar. "This will serve as a sombrilla."

She held it above her head and had to admit it made a decent sunshade.

Berto pointed to the top of the hill behind them and scrambled up. "Come on!"

"I'll follow," she called. "First, I have something to do." Solimar lowered the banana leaf and removed the rebozo. She unfurled it, held it out to the sun, and turned in a slow circle, infusing the fabric with warmth and energy until the patterns began to shimmer and pulse.

"Solimar, come take a look!" yelled Berto.

She carefully rolled the rebozo and tied it around her waist again, then headed uphill. At the crest, Solimar gasped. Nothing could have prepared her for what she saw.

The sun was low and there was more sky than earth, the clouds streaking orange and pink and violet above the great port town of Puerto Rivera on the massive Río Diablo. Far below them in the enormous horseshoe harbor, a half dozen three-masted sailing ships anchored on the outskirts. Smaller boats moored closer in. Rowboats and skiffs hugged the long wooden docks that jutted above the water.

Berto untucked his binoculars from his shirt and slowly scanned the panorama. He stopped. "El Gran Mercado. Look."

Solimar took the binoculars and tracked through the town and the harbor and farther to a massive field where hundreds of tents crowded together. She handed the binoculars back to Berto. Now she had tears in her eyes. "We're almost there," she said, smiling.

Berto nodded. "We still have a long hike tomorrow. We have to get down through these foothills, take the main road to town, and find the marketplace. Let's start now, while there's still light."

"What if we run into someone?" Solimar studied their soggy clothes, sand-caked river shoes, and the huge banana leaf. "We look like river rats."

Zarita nodded. "You don't exactly . . . blend."

Berto squinted into the binoculars again, focusing on something downhill. "I can fix that."

Solimar followed him on a narrow horse path until they came to a fenced pasture. At the far end was a small stable where two horses dangled their heads over the half doors, nodding and snuffling. A tack room sat next to the stalls. Beyond that, there was a yard, and a house, and a clothesline full of laundry.

"Berto!" said Solimar. "Do you mean to steal someone's horses?"

"Absolutely not. Horse thieves are immediately hunted down and arrested. I only intend to borrow some clothes. Wouldn't your father be grateful if it helped save the kingdom?"

"Yes," said Solimar. "And he'd repay them generously, of course. But what if someone comes out of the house and we're caught?"

Berto peered into the binoculars. "I don't think that will happen. The horses are already put to bed. And I can't see anyone out and about. Regardless, *you're* not getting caught." He handed her the binoculars. "Wait here. I'll be right back."

"Berto, no!" But before she could protest further, he was gone, running along the pasture fence and in front of the horse stalls until he reached the edge of the yard. He quickly ducked behind the bedsheets dangling from the clothesline.

Solimar grumbled and paced. Within a few minutes, though, Berto was back, balancing two pairs of boots on top of a bundle of clothes.

Solimar took the boots. "Where did you find these?"

"In front of the tack room. And that's not all. I borrowed some apples and carrots, too. Come on."

The sun had set. Solimar lowered the banana leaf and followed Berto down the horse path. They hiked until darkness crept in and they could no longer safely see the road.

Berto ducked into a heavily wooded area. "We need to stay

here until there's enough light in the morning." He plopped the bundle on the ground, apples rolling from the pile.

Lázaro stopped one with his foot.

Berto laughed. "It's all yours, Lázaro." He knelt to pick through the clothing. "The boots look a little big, but they'll be less conspicuous than the river sandals." He tossed Solimar several pairs of socks. "These will help." He stood up. "There were only work shirts, trousers, and knit caps." He handed her a long-sleeved shirt.

She held it to her chest. "That's a good thing."

Berto tilted his head and frowned. "What do you mean?" Then his eyes widened. "You're right. King Aveno's guards will be looking for the princess-to-be and her pet bird—"

Solimar nodded. "—not for two *boys*."

TWENTY-ONE

El Gran Mercado

In the faintest morning light, Solimar tied the rebozo safely under the blue work shirt, slipped Zarita into the chest pocket, and pulled a knit cap over her head and ears. She picked up the banana leaf and studied it. "I don't want to draw attention to myself. And this—"

"—basically screams, 'Look at me!'" said Zarita.

"I agree," said Berto. "To be safe, we should all try to be as inconspicuous as possible." He pointed at Zarita.

Zarita crossed her heart.

Lázaro landed on Solimar's shoulder.

She reached up to pet him. "The guards are looking for you, too. You need to hide, and no singing. You can follow us tree to tree."

Lázaro nuzzled her hand, then flew to a nearby oak, almost completely concealing himself in the leafy branches.

"It will be overcast for a few hours," said Berto. "Then we'll stay in the shade as much as possible."

Solimar tossed the banana leaf aside and followed Berto, clomping along in the boots that were still a little too large, even with extra socks.

"So, Solimar, how exactly are we going to do this? Is there a plan?" asked Berto.

Solimar's brow furrowed. "We know that my father and Campeón are both being watched. And King Aveno's guards and spies will be alerted to anyone who is curious about their whereabouts. So we can't just ask around."

Zarita popped up from the pocket. "We don't know who is friend and who is foe."

"True," said Berto. "We can't trust anyone."

"First, we need to find the tent where San Gregorio is selling their goods and watch for my father and brother," said Solimar. "Then follow them. And hopefully figure out how to get a message to them. What do you think?"

"It's as good a plan as any," said Berto.

All morning as they hiked through the foothills, they didn't pass anyone except for a farmer herding sheep and a few stray dogs. By midday, though, they had reached the road to town and encountered more foot traffic and the occasional wagon or cart.

They crossed over to the shady side of the road, but the more people they passed face-to-face, the more Solimar's confidence faded. She felt self-conscious, convinced that everyone was a spy and would recognize her. Every polite nod or cheerful hello made her panic.

For the rest of the afternoon, Solimar kept close to Berto with her head down and avoiding any eye contact with strangers. When they stopped for a moment's rest, she asked, "How much farther to Puerto Rivera?"

"It's taking longer than I thought," said Berto. "If we had horses, we'd be there by now. Don't worry. We'll make it in time."

"I hope you're right," she said. But doubts crowded her thoughts.

It was dusk by the time they reached Puerto Rivera and the center of Main Street. Berto pointed toward a half dozen young men crowded around a public notice board—the Port of Call sailings.

Solimar edged into the crowd until she was close enough to read it. She scanned down the list of ships. Her heart jumped when she saw *La Quinta*.

She hurried to Berto. "*La Quinta* sails at dawn. And they're soliciting deckhands, just like Campeón said. That means he will sneak away sometime late tonight as planned."

"Good. This way," said Berto, pointing toward the end of the street where the colored tents loomed.

Solimar froze as two of King Aveno's uniformed guards came toward them.

Berto moved closer to her and muttered, "Keep walking."

But Solimar panicked and spun around to run, bumping into a woman and upending her shopping bag. "I'm so sorry!" cried Solimar.

The guards walked by, paying no attention to her.

Berto picked up the goods and handed them back to the woman, then pulled Solimar aside. "I thought the idea was to *not* draw attention?"

Solimar's eyes darted at each person on the road. "I'm sorry. I'm just nervous. There's not much time. And King Aveno's guards could be anyone, and anywhere."

"But they're not looking for *us*," said Berto.

"Breathe in. Breathe out," whispered Zarita. "Portray calm and confidence and no one will be the wiser. Besides, people are focused on themselves."

Berto nodded. "Ditto to what she said."

Solimar took a deep breath and looked around. Everyone *did* seem to be going about their business without giving them a second look.

"Try to look . . . casual," said Berto.

"Casual," she repeated.

"Nonchalant," he added.

"Like I don't have a care in the world." She tried to smile, but it was halfhearted.

When they finally entered the main aisle of El Gran Mercado, they paused to take it all in. It was more like a grand fiesta than a grand marketplace, and the party was in full swing.

Even though it wasn't yet dark, lanterns, already aglow, crisscrossed the aisles from the tops of the tents and swayed in the gentle breeze. Guitars strummed. The delicious aroma of food cooking wafted in the air, and vendors called out to anyone walking in the aisle to buy something. El Gran Mercado was a concert of people talking, bartering, eating, laughing, and clapping to music.

Solimar relaxed a little. It was much easier to disappear within the milling crowds than it had been on the main road. Here, everyone was preoccupied. She and Berto walked up the center row slowly, stopping briefly at each booth as if they were shoppers.

A woman wearing a long apron stepped from a stall, holding a bowl of watermelon, papaya, and pineapple chunks sprinkled with chili powder and salt crystals. A bamboo pick was stuck in the pyramid of fruit. She offered it to Solimar. "For you, young man?"

Solimar's mouth watered, and her stomach cramped. She reached out to take it but remembered she had no money. Jerking her hand back, she said, "No, thank you."

"That was close," whispered Berto, taking her elbow and steering her away.

"I know," whispered Solimar. "She would have yelled *thief,* and all eyes would have been on us. Better to stay focused on the task at hand. Let's find San Gregorio's tent." Solimar stopped and slowly turned. The market was a dizzying panorama of color and people and flags. "If I could just get up higher."

When they reached the end of the aisle, Berto considered a large pile of empty crates. "I can fix that." He quickly upturned them and made a base and then stacked them against a pole in four levels in stair fashion. "I'll steady them so they don't wobble."

Solimar scrambled up and gazed across the tent tops. The market was massive, with row upon row of vendors. When she spotted San Gregorio's flag, she was overwhelmed with a yearning for home. Tears filled her eyes. "Father and Campeón," she whispered. They were so close. She clambered down. "Six rows over."

Solimar and Berto sat at one of many picnic tables crowded beneath open-air tents on a grassy area across from San Gregorio's tent. From this spot, they had a good view of who went in and out. Solimar studied their setup: the huge tent lined with shelves filled with muñecas de trapo, table upon table of butterfly-themed arts and crafts, racks of jackets, and shawls embroidered with monarchs. But she didn't see Father or Campeón.

A man carrying mesh bags filled with groceries and heading toward a food tent struggled by them. He stopped to shift the weight.

Berto jumped up. "Señor, can I help you?"

"Sí, por favor. Your kindness will be repaid."

Berto leaned toward Solimar and winked. "That's what I'm counting on. I'll be right back."

A few minutes later, he returned, grinning, with two burritos and kicking a ball in front of him.

Amazed, she shook her head. "Still borrowing things?"

"He gave me the food for helping him, and asked if I wanted the ball, too. Said it had been left behind days ago and he had no use for it. It might come in handy."

They ate quickly, keeping an eye on the San Gregorio tent.

"Any sign of your father or brother?" asked Berto.

Solimar shook her head. "So far, it's just villagers who are working and customers roaming the tent. We need to find the encampment. It would be a site where they could corral the animals away from the market but close enough to walk back and forth."

"When I helped the man with his groceries, I noticed a road behind the tents." He grabbed the ball. "I'll show you."

They slowly wandered down the road in one direction until they reached a dead end. They doubled back until they had almost reached the edge of the forest, kicking the ball between them, passing any number of campsites, until Solimar stopped and nodded to Berto.

San Gregorio's encampment was an enclave down a wide dirt path at the far end of a grassy field. The entire site was surrounded on three sides by forested hills.

At the edge of the grass, Solimar and Berto paused and kept the ball moving between them so they could get a good look at the camp.

A dozen tents dotted the site, the largest bearing the royal crest. Stakes and ropes penned the horses and donkeys in temporary corrals, and the dogs were tethered on long ropes beneath the surrounding trees. Several villagers milled about, tending a fire and feeding the animals.

Berto passed the ball to Solimar and raised his eyebrows. "Do you see them?"

She shook her head, picked up the ball, and came closer. "Don't be too obvious, but check out the other side of the road."

Berto glanced across the way, where two men sat at a tall barrel at the back of a tent. They appeared to be playing cards, but with a keen eye on the field and San Gregorio's site. A little farther away, it was the same thing—two cardplayers who were more interested in what was going on in the encampment than their game.

Berto whispered, "Aveno's guards."

Solimar pulled the knit cap lower. "Let's go somewhere else."

When they were far enough away, Solimar stopped and rubbed her forehead. "We'll never get in there unnoticed. And even if we did, Juan Pedro said there were spies everywhere.

My father thinks he's going to the secret meeting *with* Campeón tomorrow morning. But Campeón will already have left on the ship at dawn, and he's the only one who can get a message to Father. We need to intercept Campeón. If he sticks to his original plan, he will leave to board *La Quinta* tonight after Father goes to sleep."

"Won't the guards see him?" asked Berto.

Solimar shook her head. "He disguises himself and knows how to slip out without anyone noticing. And"—she paused, smiling—"there's only one road that leads to the harbor."

Solimar and Berto found a sheltered spot on the forested side of the road to the harbor.

They were hidden, but there was enough moonlight to see anyone heading their way toward the ships and docks.

Lázaro, their lookout, perched in a tree.

They'd been waiting since midnight, and with each passing minute, Solimar's hopes of diverting Campeón dwindled.

"Maybe he was caught trying to leave camp by King Aveno's guards," said Berto.

"Let's think positive," said Zarita.

Solimar shook her head. "No. He'd be extra careful tonight. He's been waiting for this chance for a long time."

As the night wore on and Campeón didn't appear, Solimar's

mind raced with all that might have happened. He *could* have changed his mind. But in her heart, she didn't think he would. Father *could* have woken as he was leaving. But that didn't seem likely. If Campeón didn't show up, then what? The worry and emotion of the last few days gripped Solimar. She sat on the ground next to a tree and leaned her head back.

"Relax," said Zarita. "Láz will alert us."

"I can't." Solimar sighed. "I'm too worried."

"Listen to the sound of my voice," said Zarita. "Imagine all your troubles on one puffy cloud, floating away from you. Isn't that lovely? Now close your eyes and breathe in to the count of four. One, two, three, four. And out—two, three, four. That's it . . ."

Zarita's voice droned on. A blanket of fatigue covered Solimar, until finally, she dozed.

She startled awake when Berto shook her arm.

"Lázaro whistled. Someone's coming."

Solimar stood up. The road was empty except for a lone figure in the distance walking toward them. The person wore rumpled work clothes and a wide-brimmed straw hat, and carried an old mesh shopping bag. It could have been a stable hand or a vendor from the marketplace. As they drew closer, Solimar didn't need to see their face to recognize who it was. Campeón's stride gave him away. She nodded to Berto.

Berto stepped into the road. "Hey there! Are you heading to *La Quinta*?"

Campeón stopped. "Hello. Did you sign up, too?"

"Yes," said Berto, then he lowered his voice. "But not for what you think. Prince Campeón, right?"

Campeón looked around to see if anyone was near. "Who are you? And how do you know my name? Did my father send you? Because—"

"No. Not your father." Berto stepped closer. "Your sister, Solimar. Come with me."

Campeón jerked back. "What is this? Some sort of trick? I have nothing of value!"

"No, no, nothing like that." Berto held his arm out to the side and whistled.

Lázaro swooped down and landed on his hand.

Campeón's eyes widened. "Lázaro! Where is she?"

Berto nodded toward the side of the road.

Solimar stepped from the bushes and pulled off the knit cap.

"Soli!" Campeón leaped to her, hugging her tight. "How? What are you doing here? Wait. Why are you dressed like that?"

She pulled him into their hiding spot behind the trees and bushes, where Zarita waited, poised on a log.

"Hi. I'm Zarita." She patted the spot next to her. "Sit down."

Campeón hesitated and looked at Berto.

"There's no time to get used to her," said Berto. "Trust us. She's a friend."

"Just listen," said Solimar. "I'll explain everything."

Campeón warily lowered himself next to a grinning Zarita.

Solimar recounted everything that had happened and what was at stake. Campeón's emotions echoed her own: the surprise about the magic, the anguish about their mother and grandmother and the hostages, the frustration and anger at King Aveno's plans to capture him and Father and Solimar, and the quiet resolve and determination to put their heads together to come up with a plan.

Campeón drew a map of the encampment and the surrounding areas in the dirt, pointing out key places and the route to the secret meeting. "We will need help. I'm going to the captain of *La Quinta*. She is fair and respected. If she could spare some sailors for a few days, Father would be indebted to her. I think this captain would welcome having a king in her good graces. Then I'll sneak back into the encampment to brief Father."

Solimar repeated everyone's roles. "Campeón, reinforcements. Berto, scouting. Lázaro and Zarita, diversionary tactics. And I will oversee and try to avoid being spotted until it's my time."

"It's a worthy strategy!" said Zarita.

"If it works, yes," said Solimar. "If not, we have lost everything."

TWENTY-TWO

Diversions and Deceptions

As the sun yawned and stretched, Berto and Solimar waited within the dense forest halfway up the hill above the royal encampment.

From there, they could see the comings and goings of the San Gregorians, and with the binoculars, they had a good view of the main aisle of the marketplace, which already buzzed with vendors and customers.

"Your brother did the honorable thing by staying," said Berto.

Solimar didn't answer but gave a slight nod. She hadn't

wanted to ruin Campeón's dream but was so grateful that he didn't hesitate to help.

"I like Prince Campeón," whispered Zarita. "He wasn't alarmed by me much."

"He liked you, too," said Solimar, blinking back tears. "He's a good brother. I suppose it will be better this way."

"It will be," said Berto. "And he'll have another chance. You'll see."

"Maybe," said Solimar, knowing that her father would never allow him to leave San Gregorio.

Berto pointed toward the camp. "It's time."

King Sebastián emerged from a tent and put on his riding gloves. He looked up at the sky as if appraising the weather.

A stable hand led Saturno to him.

Solimar wanted so much to call out and run to her father and feel the safety of his arms and hear him tell her that everything would be all right. She blew out a long frustrated breath.

"I know. It's hard to be patient," said Zarita. "Just a little longer . . ."

King Sebastián swung into his saddle and rode from the encampment and down the road. He was almost out of sight when four of Aveno's guards appeared on horseback and trotted after him.

"Right on schedule," said Berto. "They'll stay far enough behind so they won't be seen, until they reach a secluded spot. Then they'll surround and capture the king, with the intention of escorting him back to San Gregorio. On horseback and without the caravan, it will only take a few days."

"Now we have to deal with the remaining guards and spies here, or they will soon follow," said Solimar.

"And the less of them, the better," said Berto. "Plus, there's still a reward on your head."

Solimar called for Lázaro, who flew down from a nearby branch to her shoulder and began chattering.

"He wants to confirm that we're going for confusion and chaos. Right?" asked Zarita.

"Right," said Solimar. She pointed to the top of the hill. "And when you're finished, I will wait for you on the ridge." With Zarita's ribbons, she fashioned a halter around Lázaro by crisscrossing them around his chest and back.

"Perfect," said Zarita, tucking herself inside. "Like a baby in a sling. Thank goodness I'm light as a feather."

"Remember, choose your moment wisely," said Berto.

"Don't worry," said Zarita. "I'll startle the socks off them. A little creepy chanting, then the mention of a horrible curse. I got this!"

"We'll be watching your performances," said Berto, waving the binoculars.

Lázaro bowed and flew across the royal encampment, hovering in front of the guards, who were still sitting at a table pretending to play cards.

One of the guards jumped up. "That's the bird that belongs to Solimar, King Sebastián's daughter!"

"Are you sure?" asked the other.

"There's the silver band with the royal crest on its leg!"

"It's carrying . . . a doll!"

"It must be the girl's. She can't be far away."

"Follow that bird!"

Lázaro screeched and flew into the marketplace.

The guards yelled for help and chased after Lázaro. More guards joined them, in uniforms and in plain clothes. Lázaro hopped from tent pole to tent pole, then made a dive for a fruit stall.

Berto laughed and passed the binoculars to Solimar.

The woman in the fruit stall screamed and waved a towel as Lázaro leaped from bowl to bowl, eating tidbits of freshly cut fruit.

Guards overran the stall. One flung himself across a table, reaching for Lázaro. It collapsed under him, sending the fruit sliding into a messy stew.

Lázaro flew to the panadería stall next, landing on a cart of sweet rolls stacked in a beautiful tower. He tugged one from the bottom, and they all tumbled to the ground. The baker yelled and ran at him with a broom.

When Lázaro stopped at the far end of the aisle, calmly pecking at the pastry, a dozen guards surrounded him.

He flew up and over them, landing only a few feet away. He looked at them and chirped, took a few steps, stopped, and looked back at them again.

One of the guards held out his arms, blocking the others

from running forward. He looked in the direction Lázaro was headed, and pointed.

Lázaro strutted away from the marketplace, stopping every few feet to look at the pack of expectant guards who were cautiously tiptoeing after him.

"Good job, Lázaro," whispered Solimar. "He's leading them to the road. And when they're far enough away, Zarita will slip out of the sling and become animated, but not in a good way."

"Don't you wish you could see their faces when she makes her announcement?" said Berto. "Just to be clear, she can't really *do* what she's going to threaten, right?"

Solimar giggled. "You mean tell them if they continue to search for me and pledge loyalty to King Aveno, that she'll cast a spell on them so that their food will forevermore be infested with beetles and worms? No. But Lázaro will very discreetly drop a few beetles and worms in places that will guarantee they believe her."

A voice called out, "Solimar!"

She spun around to see a stable hand walking toward them, trailing two horses. He wore an oversize straw hat and held the reins of two saddled horses.

For a moment, Solimar froze. Then she ran to him and flung herself into his arms. "Father!"

He hugged her, rocking her back and forth, then held her at arm's length. "Solimar, if everything I've heard this morning is true, you have been very brave."

He looked at Berto, smiling. "And you must be the other hero in this endeavor to save our kingdom."

"Father, this is Berto," said Solimar.

Berto stood a little taller. "Rigoberto Ayala Bernal, from Valle Granada."

The king handed Berto the reins to one of the horses. "I owe you a great debt."

"Thank you, King Sebastián. It was, and is, my honor."

"And Arturo?" asked Solimar.

"He insisted on being the one to switch places with me and pose as king." He chuckled. "Thank goodness we have a similar stature. In my clothes and on my horse, he easily fooled the guards. It was a smart idea."

"Campeón thought of it," said Solimar. "Now Arturo, who they think is you, can be captured for the time being. And you can go to your meeting."

Her father sighed. "Campeón. I must admit that when he told me he had planned to leave us, I was devastated. And after what I've learned in the last few hours, I'm grateful he made the wise and responsible decision to stay. I am proud of you both. And according to the plan, I have spread the gossip that the prince has joined the crew of *La Quinta* and gone to sea. And I have acted appropriately surprised and disappointed." He put an arm around Solimar's shoulder, smoothing the rebozo. "Is this what carries the magic that King Aveno wants to harness?"

Solimar nodded.

"How have you managed to be so courageous?"

Solimar shrugged. "I gave myself permission."

He laughed. "Well, we will need a little more of that bravery before this is all said and done. But remember, Solimar, we're still in danger, especially you, and there is no guarantee this plan will work."

"I know, Father. But we have to try. For the sacred firs, and the butterflies, and for San Gregorio."

He smiled. "Truer words were never spoken. Now, I need to attend the not-so-secret meeting and hopefully form an alliance. You and Berto should head out. Campeón, the captain of *La Quinta,* and the crew are waiting on horseback at the edge of town. Do you know the spot?"

"Campeón gave us directions," said Solimar.

Father put a hand on her shoulder. "Tonight, Campeón's band will overtake the four guards who have captured Arturo-posed-as-me. I don't want you or Berto in the fray. Stay well back. Understood?"

Solimar nodded. "Understood. We will wait for you in the forest."

"With any luck, I will meet up with you tomorrow. And I'll bring any San Gregorians I can spare from the marketplace. Until then . . ." He kissed her on the forehead.

Solimar and Berto climbed into the saddles and rode away toward the top of the hill. On the ridge, they stopped.

Puerto Rivera sprawled below.

Berto lifted the binoculars, then handed them to Solimar. "Follow the harbor road to a cluster of trees on the right."

Solimar peered through the lenses until she found Campeón and a crew of sailors, waiting on horseback. "I see them."

"I'll ride a minute ahead of you, in case any of Aveno's guards are still about," said Berto.

Solimar nodded. "I'll wait for Lázaro and Zarita. They should be back soon, then I'll follow."

When Berto was far enough away, she emerged from the shade of the forest. A long trail of butterflies flew above her. Several spiraled down, fluttering around Solimar. She opened the rebozo. The fabric pulsed, calling forth the ancient songs. A flutter of butterflies emerged from the rebozo, circling and darting in joyous flight, then finally swooping away with the others.

She lifted the rebozo in front of her, studying it.

Only one blink of shimmer remained.

While she waited for Lázaro and Zarita, Solimar hugged the rebozo to her chest.

Could she protect it until she reached the castle? And even so, would it have the strength to survive the ordeal ahead?

TWENTY-THREE

The Near Future

Three days later in San Gregorio, Solimar sat on a horse in the courtyard in front of the castle.

An early morning drizzle dampened the blanket that had been draped like a cape around her. She slumped forward, her hands bound with rope to the saddle horn. Lázaro perched on her shoulder and Zarita burrowed in a pocket.

Berto was on the horse next to her, his hands tied in the same way.

Four uniformed riders, wearing King Aveno's colors surrounded them.

"Berto, no matter what happens, I want to say I'm sorry for all the trouble," said Solimar. "And how things turned out."

He shrugged. "Don't be sorry. I chose to come."

"You could have refused to take me downriver."

He gave her a lopsided smile. "It was all worth it, just for the chance we might save our homelands."

"I will never forget your sacrifice," said Solimar.

"Me either," whispered Zarita from her pocket.

From Solimar's shoulder, Lázaro peeped.

Berto raised his chin toward the castle. "I wish I could say I can fix that, but . . ."

Shouts rang out from the tower.

"We've been spotted," said Berto. "No turning back."

Solimar murmured, "No turning back."

From inside the castle, a tramping of boots echoed as an entourage of guards rushed out to meet them. In the plaza, they stood in a formation—two rigid lines, creating an aisle that reached almost to Solimar and Berto.

King Aveno appeared between the ranks and sauntered forward until he stood in front of them.

"Where are King Sebastián and the prince?" he demanded.

"We have not yet seen the king or the guards who captured him," said the rider next to Berto. "And we heard a rumor that the prince joined the crew of the ship *La Quinta*, which sailed this morning."

King Aveno smiled. "Even better if it is true. The kingdom

is now more vulnerable. And no matter about King Sebastián. Soon enough, Solimar will tell me everything I want to know about her father."

He snapped his fingers.

A guard from the formation stepped forward.

"Take the river boy," he ordered, "and put him with the other hostages."

The guard took the reins of Berto's horse and led it away.

King Aveno pointed to the rider next to Solimar. "Help her down." He nodded to the others. "Then off to the stables, all of you. Tend to the horses."

"Right away, sir!"

"Aye, aye, sir."

"Yes, sir!"

One of them quickly slid from his saddle and untied Solimar's hands so she could dismount.

As the riders departed, King Aveno turned to Solimar. "We need to talk." He flipped his hands toward the gray sky. "But the weather this morning isn't very conducive to the conversation I want to have." He grinned. "Luckily, sun is predicted this afternoon. So we will have a little event with everyone in attendance. And you and I will be the stars of the show."

"I'd like to see my mother," said Solimar.

"All in good time," said King Aveno. "Right now you'll be escorted to your room." Two guards stepped from the formation, stood on either side of her, and ushered her into the castle and through the main entry hall.

Solimar walked as slowly as possible, hoping to glimpse her mother, Abuela, Señor Verde, or anyone she knew. But she saw no one. She climbed the grand staircase to the second floor. As she walked down the long hall to her room, the weight of what might happen grew heavier. What would she reveal to King Aveno?

When she reached her room, one of the guards opened the door, nodded for her to go inside, and pulled it closed. A key rattled and turned in the lock, making sure she couldn't escape.

Solimar changed into dry clothes and flung herself on her bed. Zarita and Lázaro huddled next to her.

"You've got this," whispered Zarita.

All morning, the rain came down. With each passing hour, Solimar grew more and more apprehensive. She jumped when she heard a loud knock. Someone turned the key and the door swung open.

Señora Batista stood before her, holding a tray. A guard shadowed her.

Solimar rushed to her. "Señora Batista! Oh, I am so glad to see you! Where is my mother? And Abuela? Are they safe? Tell me."

Señora Batista briskly walked past her into the room and set the tray on the small table. "I'm sorry, Solimar, I'm not allowed to talk right now. I am only permitted to deliver your lunch. Why don't you eat? I made one of my sandwiches, the kind where I slip a little something savory between the ham and cheese. I remember how you *always* look forward to that."

"Enough!" said the guard.

Señora Batista winked at Solimar, then quickly left, followed by the guard, who shut and locked the door.

Zarita, who had been lying on the bed and pretending to be lifeless, sat up. "What was that all about?"

"It's an old joke. Señor Verde called Señor Batista's sandwiches mountainous and teased that he always expected to find one of her cook's journals between . . ." She stopped. And rushed to the table, lifting the domed lid on the tray. The sandwich was indeed mountainous. She looked closer.

Carefully, she removed the bread, lettuce, avocado, and tomato. Between the ham and cheese was a folded piece of paper. She smoothed it out to find a note in Abuela's handwriting.

Don't eat the pastries.

By two o'clock the sky was unapologetically sunny.

From the courtyard, trumpeters played a fanfare calling everyone to the festivities.

Solimar stood on her bedroom balcony, warming the rebozo and hoping it would be enough sunshine to sustain the remaining butterfly. How many questions would King Aveno ask? Would they drain the strength of the one she carried? Her heart ached at the thought that it might not survive. Gazing toward the oyamel forest in the distance, she begged the ancestral spirits for help.

When the guards knocked on the door, she draped the rebozo over her shoulders, tucked Zarita in her pocket, and called Lázaro to her shoulder. She held her head high as she followed the guards down the hall and the grand staircase, where they paused on the landing.

Below, the main hall was a mass of confusion. Guards crowded around the large entry table that was now covered with dozens of three-tiered trays filled with Señora Batista's delectable pastries in individual servings: coconut cakes, caramel flan, pineapple empanadas, cinnamon cookies, powdered sugar tea cakes. As the trumpeters continued blaring, the guards jostled to get close enough to grab a sweet on their way out.

The soldiers on either side of Solimar took her elbows and whisked her down the stairs and through the crowd, yelling, "Make way!"

At the door, they found themselves face-to-face with Señora Batista. She held out a tray. "¡Señores!" she said, smiling. "Wouldn't you like one of my famous powdered sugar cookies before you leave?"

Their mouths watered. They looked at one another, shrugged, and popped one into their mouths.

In the courtyard, a makeshift theater had been set up with chairs arranged around a stage. Huge awnings had been draped pole to pole above the audience area to provide shade. The stage, though, was bathed in sunshine.

The musicians stood on either end of the platform, trumpeting.

King Aveno stepped up and positioned himself center stage.

Juan Pedro followed and stood next to him.

The guards marched Solimar to King Aveno's side.

Solimar gasped as a contingent of guards escorted her grandmother, her mother, Berto, and the other hostages to the front rows. The castle staff and the villagers, who had not traveled with the caravan, filed into the seats behind them. The guards took the remaining seats. It was a full house.

King Aveno spread his arms wide. "Silence. No one speaks except me!"

The audience quieted.

King Aveno grinned. "Welcome, everyone. Solimar of San Gregorio has a gift to share with me. The gift of prophecy! She can tell the immediate future. Isn't that true, Solimar?"

"Yes," she said.

Surprised murmuring spread through the audience.

King Aveno barked, "Quiet! Now, Solimar, tell me, who is my most ardent ally?"

She blurted, "Juan Pedro, formerly of San Gregorio."

Juan Pedro stood a little taller.

"And is it true that your brother has joined the crew of the ship *La Quinta*?"

"Yes."

"Wonderful. Next, will your father sell me a thousand acres today?"

"No. Not today."

"Will he sell them to me tomorrow?" asked King Aveno.

"No."

King Aveno's voice tensed. "What *is* he willing to sell me?"

"A thousand flour tortillas. Nothing more. Nothing less," she said.

A smattering of giggles ran through the audience.

Solimar looked at Abuela and nodded.

Abuela stood, held a brass bell above her head, and enthusiastically rang it.

Señora Batista, who sat at the end of the front row near a pole, pulled a rope. The awnings above the audience collapsed, spilling all manner of household items into the laps of the audience: feather dusters, wooden spoons, tea towels, bonnets, house slippers, umbrellas, mittens, and assorted laundry.

Everyone who had been forewarned about the pastries and had not eaten them laughed as each guard picked up an inanimate object—and immediately fell hopelessly in love with it. At least for a few weeks, they would be as lovestruck and preoccupied as Serafina, whose sweetheart was a green woolen sock.

King Aveno's eyes bulged, and his cheeks puffed. He bellowed, "Attention! Attention! Or you will be arrested for insubordination!"

But it did no good. The guards ignored him, enamored of their new affections.

King Aveno's face reddened. "Solimar, where is King Sebastián?"

"He is here on the castle grounds, waiting and watching from the barbican tower."

Juan Pedro smirked. "I knew she couldn't help but answer."

King Aveno cupped his hands around his mouth and yelled, "Come out and join us, King Sebastián! Or your family is at risk!"

Solimar looked toward the gateway.

A hush settled.

The plodding of hoofbeats echoed on cobblestones, growing louder. All eyes shifted toward the gateway and the solitary figure of King Sebastián on horseback, riding toward them.

Prince Campeón trailed him.

Two more riders followed.

Then four abreast. And four more.

Row upon row of allies on horseback continued—the captain of *La Quinta* and her crew, the San Gregorians the king could spare from the marketplace, the leaders of the alliance kingdoms, and their entourages.

"Solimar!" seethed King Aveno. "I demand to know the meaning of this. What are their intentions?"

Solimar's words flew. "To display the unity of the newly formed permanent alliance of the kingdoms of the northern lands, pledging support to one another against you and the wanton stripping of the oyamel forests. And dedication to protecting the habitat of monarch butterflies. Their intention is to arrest you for blackmail and kidnapping."

"Where are the rest of my guards from the marketplace?"

"They have deserted and betrayed you."

King Aveno's eyes darted from her father to all the riders to his inept guards.

"If only you knew how to escape and disappear," said Solimar.

He grabbed Solimar's hand and jerked her closer. "Yes! Of course! I will ask you and you must answer. How can I vanish so they'll never find me?"

She blurted, "Through the power of the ancestral spirits, by breaking the bond between me, the chosen benevolent courier, and the rebozo."

Juan Pedro pointed to the rebozo. "You must take it from her! It's the only way out."

"But I must warn you," Solimar said, "it is not advisable to take this course of—"

King Aveno grabbed the rebozo from Solimar and quickly tied it in a knot around his waist. He laughed. "I knew this little gift of yours would be advantageous!"

From Solimar's pocket, Zarita's voice lilted in singsong. "Rage, madness, impending doom. It's not nice to anger the departed. No, siree. Wrath is no picnic. . . ."

The sky darkened, and a wind stirred and steadily grew.

The oyamel forest trembled, moaned, and whined. Leaves, branches, and debris whipped about as everyone in the audience ducked for protection.

Lázaro squawked and tugged at Solimar's skirt.

She ran from the platform and huddled on the ground.

From the forest, a dark tornado-like cloud raced toward the stage. Juan Pedro and King Aveno held on to each other in an attempt to withstand the fierce gale. The wind roared.

The swirling wind descended upon King Aveno and Juan Pedro. A dissonant chorus began, the voices jarring and growing louder and louder.

Solimar shuddered and covered her ears.

The funnel lifted away, growing smaller and smaller until it vanished.

When the wind and the world quieted, King Aveno and Juan Pedro were nowhere to be seen. All that remained were their boots and Solimar's crumpled rebozo.

She ran to the platform and inspected the fabric. One winged pattern, faded and barely visible, was wedged among the wrinkles. Had King Aveno's questions drained the strength from the last butterfly's life? "No . . ." she whimpered.

A wave of butterflies erupted from the oyamel forest. They dove and swooped around Solimar.

"I'm sorry," she cried.

The ancient song began, beautiful and melodic. The butterflies lifted the fabric, turning it around and around in the sun, and waving it so that it rippled until the creases fell away.

As the rebozo drifted downward, a tiny speck shimmered and grew brighter. One monarch emerged, circling! Solimar held up her hand, and the last one she protected landed on her finger, then flew away to join the others in the oyamel forest.

The rebozo drifted from the sky and onto her shoulders.

Villagers rushed forward and surrounded Solimar, peppering her with questions.

"Will I win the footrace tomorrow?"

"Will I pass my exam?"

"Will I receive a horse for my birthday?"

Solimar waited, just to be sure. Nothing came to her! "I have no idea."

"But can't you tell the future?"

"Heaven's no!" she answered. "It was just a little commonsense clairvoyance and the power of suggestion to fool King Aveno."

TWENTY-FOUR

Princess of the World

Two weeks later, Solimar stood at the top of the veranda with her quinceañera court lined up two-by-two on the steps below her, ready to descend to the royal garden in a grand entrance.

Señora Vega and the other seamstresses came up the line, fluffing the skirts of the dresses, including María's turquoise one and Estela's pistachio. They reached Solimar and fussed over her new coral gown, which was as beautiful as the first one, and then they took a few steps back to admire it.

"Thank you," said Solimar. "I don't know how you all made another in such a short time. You saved the day."

"It was the least we could do for the heroine who saved the kingdom," said Señora Vega. "Otherwise, we might be sewing for King Aveno. And that would have been a sad state. But let's not talk about that on such a glorious evening!"

Lázaro flew to Solimar's shoulder, his feathers embellished with ribbons, courtesy of Zarita.

Señora Vega handed the almost-new princess a bouquet of flowers and tulle in which Zarita was nestled, the doll now wearing a gown that matched Solimar's.

"Muchas gracias, Señora Vega," squealed Zarita. "I love what you did with the overskirt and the bodice. And the circular flounce on the sleeve is divine. Do I look lovely?"

"Of course," said Señora Vega. "I knew exactly what you would like."

"Zarita, you *talk* with Señora Vega?" asked Solimar.

"Didn't I tell you? I speak seamstress," said Zarita. "Now promise not to put me down for a minute tonight, especially during the dancing."

Solimar smiled. "I promise." She looked out over the festivities below. It *was* a glorious night. Lanterns glowed, the village flags fluttered in a gentle evening breeze, and violins hummed as the musicians tuned them. In the garden, an enormous dance floor had been laid, now empty except for one unoccupied chair for the shoe ceremony.

The entire kingdom had gathered to watch her become a princess of the world, and be officially crowned Princess Solimar Socorro Reyes Guadalupe of San Gregorio. Her eyes welled with tears of gratitude for a day that only a few weeks ago she didn't want to happen.

A burst of laughter erupted from a group of young men and women surrounding Campeón. He was leaving in a few weeks for Puerto Rivera to rejoin *La Quinta* and travel the world. Everyone wanted to wish him well and say good-bye. Campeón was more animated than Solimar had ever seen him and holding everyone captive. Most likely by recounting the story one more time about how they—Solimar, Berto, and Campeón—saved the kingdom.

The orchestra started the procession music. King Sebastián and Queen Rosalinda walked to the center of the dance floor. He carried a shoe box, and she held a satin pillow cradling a crown. Solimar couldn't find where it was written that *only* her father should participate in the shoe ceremony. Or that only the king could crown her. So she asked for *both* of her parents to do the honors.

Her court proceeded down the steps, the girls and boys wearing wreaths of dahlias and ivy. Berto looked a little stiff and uncomfortable in his white suit and vest but stood tall and proud. Solimar had been overjoyed when he agreed to come and bring his mother and his sisters.

After the entire court formed a semicircle around the empty chair on the dance floor, King Sebastián raised his arm and the crowd hushed.

The orchestra began a dramatic and triumphant march.

Slowly, step-by-step, Solimar descended to the dance floor and her designated spot. With her skirt and its many layers of tulle, she carefully sat down, but one of the chair's legs was shorter than the other. It rocked back and forth, and for a moment, Solimar teetered.

Berto stepped up. "I can fix that," he whispered, pulling a handkerchief from his pocket, folding it into a wedge, and sliding it under the chair leg.

Solimar grinned.

The king knelt in front of Solimar, slipped off her flat shoes of childhood, and opened the shoe box. He fitted and tied the high-heeled shoes that symbolized her bridge into womanhood—a fancy wedge version of an all-terrain sandal.

The queen, with tears in her eyes, fastened the crown on Solimar's head.

Everyone in attendance erupted in applause and cheers!

Her father held out his arms for the first dance.

As they waltzed, he said, "This is the happiest of days for me. And much of it is because of you, Solimar. Why did you risk so much?"

"For San Gregorio, our heart and our home."

His eyes brimmed, and he nodded. "Speaking of homes. We are officially adopting Valle Granada as part of the kingdom of San Gregorio. They are no longer kingdom-less. And we're investing in a reservoir system to help Berto bring the river water to their valley."

"That's wonderful! But, Father, I'd also like to explore the possibility of using the river as a faster route to the port . . . someday," said Solimar.

The king nodded. "That would benefit San Gregorio and Valle Granada. Did you know that pomegranates have medicinal uses, proving beneficial in treating fevers? And the fruit juice is an age-old remedy for memory loss. Abuela is thrilled."

Solimar glanced to the side of the dance floor, where Abuela, Doña Flor, and Berto's mother had their heads together, talking. Solimar smiled. "Of course she is."

"I want to hear more," said King Sebastián. "But first things first." He stopped dancing and searched the dance floor. "Where is Campeón? He and I made an important decision last night, but he wants to be the one to tell you. Here comes Señor Verde. Let me hand you off to him for a few minutes, and I'll find Campeón."

Señor Verde cut in. "Oh, the day we've been waiting for! It's so lovely. By now, of course, everyone knows you fooled King Aveno. And you were brilliant. But I've been puzzling over something. Tell me how, exactly, did a vicious whirlwind come forth from the forest at that precise moment? Was that somehow your doing, too? You know how I love these little tidbits of information."

"Um . . . well . . . I . . ." Solimar hesitated.

"Excuse me, Señor Verde." Campeón took Solimar in his

arms and swept her across the dance floor. "I saved you from the Shadow!"

"Thank you! What am I going to do without you?" she said, laughing but not entirely joking. When she looked at his face and how happy he was, she set aside for the moment how much she would miss him after he left. "Now, what is this very important decision Father mentioned?"

Campeón laughed. "First, congratulations, Soli. This is a great party. You're officially royalty, and it suits you. You were born to lead. And that brings me to the news." He raised his eyebrows, teasing. "Are you sure you want to know?"

"Of course! Tell me!"

He stopped waltzing, took her hand, and led her from the dance floor to a nearby stone bench, where he faced her.

Campeón took a deep breath and smiled. "As you know, I'm leaving on *La Quinta* when they dock again. I signed on for four years. I'm going to talk Father into creating a transport fleet for San Gregorio, although he doesn't know it yet. If we can sell goods in one port, we can export and import from around the world."

"Is that the news?"

Campeón shook his head. "As you're aware, in San Gregorio only a prince can become king. So Father and I signed legal papers last night. While I'm gone, you will be the prince regent of San Gregorio.

"The what?"

"Prince regent. It means prince in the absence of a sovereign."

Solimar's heart beat a little faster. "You and Father can do that?"

"We can, and we did. And that will make you first in line to the throne. Father is planning to step down in three years when you turn eighteen. So, at that time, you would become the *king* regent until I return from my travels." He grinned and winked. "That is . . . *if* I return."

"You're a princess, almost a prince, and the king-to-be all in one day!" cried Zarita.

Lázaro took to the sky twirling and whistling.

Solimar studied Campeón's face to make sure he wasn't joking.

"I will have a say?" she asked quietly.

He nodded. "Yes, Soli. You will have a very big say."

She murmured, "King Solimar."

"I like the sound of it," he said.

Solimar looked around the festivities. She spotted Abuela, who blew her a kiss.

She found her father and mother, who waved and smiled.

Solimar hugged Campeón. "I like the sound of it, too!"

Long Live the Butterfly

I grew up in the San Joaquin Valley of California and often visited the Central Coast on weekends and vacations. I also visited the Pismo Beach Butterfly Grove when the eucalyptus trees were covered in overwintering monarchs. It was an unforgettable, awe-inspiring experience.

Monarchs from west of the Rocky Mountains primarily overwinter in California, landing in pine, cypress, and eucalyptus trees along the Central Coast. But those are only a small portion of the monarchs that migrate. The majority come from east of the Rocky Mountains in the United States and Canada, like those in *Solimar*, and overwinter in the mountains of Central Mexico, almost exclusively in oyamel fir forests. Here is more information on monarch butterflies.

Why are Monarchs Important?

Monarch butterflies are pollinators, just like bees, birds, bats, beetles, wasps, and small mammals. As they travel from one flowering plant to another, they carry and leave behind pollen, which contains genetic material that enables plants to reproduce. This generates more flowering plants and trees that include fruits, vegetables, and nuts—all critical food sources.

Picky Eaters

Monarch butterflies need milkweed and nectar plants to survive. Adult butterflies drink nectar from flowering plants, which gives them the energy they need to migrate. And the females lay their eggs on milkweed leaves so that when the caterpillars hatch, food is at the ready! In the wild, native milkweed is the only food the caterpillars will eat, and they'll often eat ten or more milkweed leaves a day for about two weeks.

A Place to Hang

When a caterpillar is about to enter the chrysalis stage, it doesn't usually stay on the milkweed leaf. It finds a spot protected from wind and rain on which to attach. Chrysalises have been found dangling from all sorts of things, including other plants, ladders, window sills, trees, grates, screens, the sides of a shed, and wood piles. It will take another few weeks before a butterfly emerges. Then, it will feed on a wide range of nectar-rich flowering plants, beginning the butterfly life cycle again.

A Threatened Existence

Sadly, the monarch population has been diminishing. There are many reasons for this, including habitat loss and over-use of pesticides along the butterflies' migratory routes in the United States and Canada, which reduces the amount of nectar plants and milkweed that the butterflies need for survival and reproduction. The overwintering grounds in the oyamel fir forests of Mexico are also in trouble due to logging and wildfires. Thankfully, efforts are being made to protect them.

How to Create a Haven for Monarchs

Consider a butterfly garden for your patio, yard, school, or community. Choose a spot that is mostly sunny and not too windy. Water it regularly and keep some areas of the ground damp, or have a shallow bowl with soil, rocks, and a little water. Monarch butterflies need moisture.

Plant native milkweed in clumps of six to eight plants. When the caterpillars hatch, they will need lots of leaves to eat. There are many different types of milkweed, so you may need to call or visit a nursery to find out what type is native to your area, and when to cut it back or replant.

Adult monarchs drink nectar, so don't forget to add some nectar plants! Monarchs and other pollinators are attracted to bright, colorful blooms. Plant a variety of flowers that are nectar-rich such as lantana, echinacea, yarrow, Mexican sunflower, verbena, and others. Cluster the nectar plants, which will make it easier for the butterflies to find them.

Find Out More and Have Fun

Search online for information about monarch butterflies, butterfly conservancies, how to participate in a butterfly count, and butterfly fun facts, such as: Did you know that they taste with their feet? Or that their scientific name is Danaus plexippus, which means "sleepy transformation"? Or that they have successfully hatched on the International Space Station?

Spread the Word

Give native milkweed- and flower-seed packets or milkweed plants as gifts.

As you can see, monarch butterfly migration is a mystery and a miracle, and it's significant to the natural world. So let's all try to help.

!Viva la mariposa!

Pam Muñoz Ryan

Acknowledgments

I have immeasurable gratitude for my editor on this book, Samantha McFerrin, whose patience and dedication ushered the story to completion, and for her assistant, Andrew Elmers, for behind-the-scenes support. Thank you to Sara Liebling, managing editor, and copy editors Jody Corbett, Mark Steven Long, Ariela Rudy Zaltzman, and Harriet Sigerman.

Jacqueline Alcántara, illustrator, brought *Solimar* to life. I am grateful for her particular magic, as well as the talent of the design team, especially Joann Hill, Shelby Kahr, and Jackie Lai.

I could not have introduced *Solimar* to the world without those in the Disney publicity and marketing departments:

Danielle DiMartino, Holly Nagel, Dina Sherman, LaToya Maitland, Maddie Hughes, Marina Shults, Ian Byrne, Andrew Sansone, Kyle Wilson, and Seale Ballenger. And a special thanks to Zak Gezon and Leslie Huetter at Disney Conservation for their careful vetting and resources.

I never want to miss an opportunity to thank my benevolent couriers, the booksellers, who continue to put my books into readers' hands.

As always, big hugs to my family for understanding the life of a writer.